AROUND CHI-TOWN

News flash!

February: Even though new King Daniel is thoroughly ensconced in Altaria's royal palace, the Connelly family is once again making Chicago headlines. Informed sources tell me that a female Special Investigative Unit detective has been seen in and around the Connelly offices and lakeside retreat. And she's being squired about by Brett Connelly himself.

Does Chicago's newest most eligible bachelor need a bodyguard? And just how much protection can the dainty Detective Delgado provide, anyway?

Emma Rosemere Connelly, the former princess of Altaria, denies reports that the investigation is somehow connected to the new royal family in her island homeland. But this reporter will search the globe to bring you the truth.

In another mystery, yours truly has been baffled that man-about-town Brett has been absent from the social scene of late. Well, now rumor has it that he bagged last night's gala for a trip to Baby World, the area's largest baby-supply store.

For a man who's sported the city's most glamorous women on his arm, he sure looks odd holding a gingham teddy bear. What gives, Brett? Is someone hiding your little secret?

Now there's a case Detective Delgado can investigate!

Dear Reader,

Escape the winter doldrums by reading six new passionate, powerful and provocative romances from Silhouette Desire!

Start with our MAN OF THE MONTH, *The Playboy Sheikh*, the latest SONS OF THE DESERT love story by bestselling author Alexandra Sellers. Also thrilling is the second title in our yearlong continuity series DYNASTIES: THE CONNELLYS. In *Maternally Yours* by Kathie DeNosky, a pleasure-seeking tycoon falls for a soon-to-be mom.

All you readers who've requested more titles in Cait London's beloved TALLCHIEFS miniseries will delight in her smoldering *Tallchief: The Hunter*. And more great news for our loyal Desire readers—a *brand-new* five-book series featuring THE TEXAS CATTLEMAN'S CLUB, subtitled THE LAST BACHELOR, launches this month. In *The Millionaire's Pregnant Bride* by Dixie Browning, passion erupts between an oil executive and secretary who marry for the sake of her unborn child.

A single-dad surgeon meets his match in *Dr. Desirable*, the second book of Kristi Gold's MARRYING AN M.D. miniseries. And Kate Little's *Tall, Dark & Cranky* is an enchanting contemporary version of *Beauty and the Beast*.

Indulge yourself with all six of these exhilarating love stories from Silhouette Desire!

Enjoy!

Joan Marlow Golan

Joan Marlow Golan
Senior Editor, Silhouette Desire

Please address questions and book requests to:
Silhouette Reader Service
U.S.: 3010 Walden Ave., P.O. Box 1325, Buffalo, NY 14269
Canadian: P.O. Box 609, Fort Erie, Ont. L2A 5X3

Maternally Yours
KATHIE DeNOSKY

Published by Silhouette Books
America's Publisher of Contemporary Romance

Special thanks and acknowledgment are given to Kathie DeNosky for her contribution to the DYNASTIES: THE CONNELLYS series.

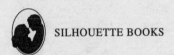 SILHOUETTE BOOKS

ISBN 0-373-76418-9

MATERNALLY YOURS

Visit Silhouette at www.eHarlequin.com

Printed in U.S.A.

Books by Kathie DeNosky

KATHIE DeNOSKY

lives in deep southern Illinois with her husband and three children. After reading and enjoying Silhouette books for many years, she is ecstatic about being able to share her stories with others as a Silhouette Desire author. Writing highly sensual stories with a generous amount of humor, Kathie's books have appeared on the Waldenbooks bestseller list. She enjoys going to rodeos, traveling to research settings for her books and listening to country music. She often starts her day at 2:00 a.m. so she can write without interruption, before the rest of the family is up and about. You may write to Kathie at: P.O. Box 2064, Herrin, Il 62948-5264.

MEET THE CONNELLYS

Wealthy, Powerful and Rocked by Scandal,
Betrayal...and Passion!

Who's Who in *Maternally Yours*

Brett Connelly—This playboy's not ready for the wife,
2.2 kids, the minivan and the white picket fence…or is
he?

Elena Delgado—She'll do anything to protect her unborn
child.

Drew Connelly—Brett's older twin—by fifteen minutes.
He's taught his younger bro a thing or two about
life…and love.

Seth Connelly—He can argue any position in a court of
law, but what's this half brother's place in the Connelly
clan?

Emma and Grant Connelly—The former princess
and brash American beat the odds. Their love match is
thirty-five years old…and still going strong.

Jennifer Anderson—Emma's personal secretary. She
gives Elena a crash course on single motherhood.

Princess Catherine—Events in her kingdom of Altaria
prevent her from visiting her American cousins.

Albert Dessage—Elena's European counterpart; he'll
stop at nothing till he uncovers the betrayal and scandal
in Altaria.

One

Elena Delgado pressed a shaky hand to her stomach, took a deep breath and slowly got to her feet. She closed her eyes and leaned against the side of the rest room stall. The nausea wasn't supposed to last all day. If it was, they would have called it something besides morning sickness. But she'd been ill almost from the instant the test stick turned blue.

She didn't mind in the least. She'd gladly go through whatever it took to complete this pregnancy successfully. She bit her lower lip and took another deep breath. This was her last hope of having her own child, of holding it and loving it with every fiber of her being—she simply couldn't afford another trip to the sperm bank. Not financially. Not emotionally.

When her stomach finally settled down, she pulled the door open and walked over to the vanity. The click of her black medium-heeled pumps striking the tiled floor echoed through the empty room. She shivered at the hollow loneliness of the sound.

Tears filled her eyes as she looked at herself in the mirror above the bank of sinks. She'd been alone all of her life. So why was she feeling so lonely now?

Disgusted with herself, Elena jerked paper towels from the dispenser on the wall and held them under the faucet, then pressed the cool wetness to her flushed cheeks. Her unstable emotions had to be caused by the hormonal changes from her pregnancy. That was the only thing it could be.

Otherwise Elena Delgado never cried. Ever.

She finished wiping away the last of the tears, draped her coat over her arm, then checked her watch. Groaning, she quickly grabbed her shoulder bag, said a silent prayer that her queasy stomach would remain calm for the next hour and walked out into the stylish reception area of Connelly Tower.

Heading for the elevators, she shook her head. She hated to be late for anything. It was rude and inconsiderate to keep people waiting. She shifted from one foot to the other as she impatiently waited for an elevator. Just one more slowdown in a day that had been filled with a series of delays and frustrations.

She'd awakened this morning to find that sometime during the night the ancient furnace in her building had finally given up the fight against Chicago's cold, hard winters and died. It had taken her twice as long to get ready for work because she couldn't stop shivering. Then she'd gone out to find that her car wouldn't start, forcing her to walk six blocks in the frigid February temperature to catch the L.

The polished brass doors of the elevator finally swished open and Elena hurriedly stepped inside. She pressed the button to the seventeenth floor, and as it began to move, she closed her eyes against a wave of nausea. Express elevators should be outlawed, she decided as the rapid ascent played havoc with her already iffy stomach.

When it eased to a stop a few seconds later and the doors opened, she stepped out into the plushly carpeted corridor on shaky legs. After she met with Brett Connelly to arrange interviews with the rest of the Connelly family, she would spend the weekend trying to feel human again. But when she left, she would take the stairs.

Brett Connelly tapped the highly polished surface of his mahogany desk with his fountain pen. Glancing at his watch for the third time in as many minutes, he resumed staring out the window at the early-evening shadows covering Lake Michigan. He hated to be kept waiting. If the detective investigating the attempted murder of his older brother, Daniel, didn't show up damned quick, Brett was calling it a day. Babe didn't like him to be late getting home from work. In fact, he'd be lucky if she didn't destroy some of his things to get back at him. She'd done that several times already.

The intercom on the corner of his desk suddenly buzzed, interrupting his thoughts. "Yes, Fiona?"

"Your four o'clock appointment has finally arrived, Mr. Connelly."

"Thank you. Send her in." As an afterthought, he added, "If you'd like, you can leave now."

"Thank you, Mr. Connelly. I'll see you on Monday. Have a nice weekend."

"You, too, Fiona."

Seconds later his office door opened, and a young woman with shoulder-length, tawny-brown hair walked into the room. Brett couldn't keep from staring. This was the hotshot detective from the Special Investigative Unit of the Chicago Police Department?

Whoa, baby! He'd been expecting some middle-aged battle-ax who looked like a man and had a hard-as-nails attitude. Instead they'd sent a petite woman who had to be somewhere in her midtwenties and could put beauty queens to shame with her looks. He made a mental note to call and thank his father for assigning him the task of liaison between his family and the police.

Brett rose to his feet as his gaze zeroed in on her left hand to see if she wore a wedding band. She didn't.

Sending a silent thank-you to the powers that be, he rounded the desk, treated her to his most charming smile—the smile that had kept his social calendar filled since his sophomore year in high school—and extended his hand. "I'm Brett Connelly, Vice President of Public Relations. And you are?"

She quickly shook his hand but didn't return his smile. "I'm SIU Detective Elena Delgado. Sorry I'm late, Mr. Connelly."

She wasn't offering an explanation for her tardiness, and Brett wasn't asking for one. He was too preoccupied with the tingling sensation running from his palm, up his arm and warming his chest.

"Since we'll be working so closely together, please call me Brett, Ms. Delgado," he said, rubbing his thumb over the silky skin on the back of her hand.

She dropped his hand, and the look she gave him indicated that she hadn't been the least bit affected by his never-fail smile or his touch. At least not the way he'd been affected by hers.

"Shall we get down to business, Mr. Connelly?" she asked politely.

Her no-nonsense demeanor certainly went with her job. But it wasn't often that he encountered a female he couldn't charm. He took it as a personal challenge.

As she continued to gaze at him expectantly, he noticed something about her that had escaped him when she'd first entered the room. Elena Delgado looked tired. Very tired. Dark circles smudged the pale skin beneath her chocolate-brown eyes, and her voice sounded extremely weary. Maybe that had something to do with her no-nonsense attitude and refusal to use his first name.

Whatever the reason, something about her stoic demeanor urged him to take up the gauntlet and improve her mood. He checked his watch. It was dinnertime and he was already late getting home. Daniel and his wife, Erin, were safely hidden from any further attempts on Daniel's life in the tiny island country of Altaria, so there was no immediate threat to his brother on that front. And Babe would treat him to the cold shoulder now, anyway. In fact, she'd probably already started destroying the living room. Being an hour or two later wouldn't make much difference.

Besides, Elena looked as if she could use something to lift her spirits. What better way than spending an evening out on the town?

"I was just getting ready to leave for the day," he said, walking over to remove his suit jacket from the brass coat tree in the corner. Shrugging into it, he reached for his leather overcoat. "Why don't we discuss the details of the interviews over dinner?"

She shook her head, and if the expression on her lovely face was any indication, it wasn't going to be easy changing her mind. "I'd rather not, Mr. Connelly."

He wasn't about to let that deter him. "I skipped breakfast and worked through lunch," he said truthfully. "It's dinnertime and I'm hungry." He smiled. "And I'm betting you are, too."

Her stomach chose that moment to rumble, making any protest she might have had ineffective. Her cheeks colored a pretty pink. He hadn't seen a woman blush like that in years.

Brett chuckled. "Then it's settled." He pulled on his overcoat and placed his hand lightly at the small of her back to usher her to the door. "We'll talk over dinner."

She didn't look happy, but Brett took it as a positive sign when she allowed him to steer her to the elevators. The swift ride down to the basement parking garage was a silent one and he began to wonder if he was losing his touch. By the time the doors opened, she looked positively miserable about being in his company.

"I'll bring you back to pick up your car," he said as they stepped out into the parking area.

"My car wouldn't start this morning," she said, sounding even more tired than before. "I took the L."

"Well, you're not taking it home," he said emphatically. Police detective or not, he didn't like the idea of a woman riding the elevated train alone at night. It just wasn't safe. Before she could protest, he quickly led her to his black Jaguar and opened the passenger door. "Do you like Italian food?"

She practically collapsed into the bucket seat before she answered. "Yes, I normally love Italian food, but I don't think it would be—"

"Good. Then Italian it is," he said, closing the door. When she glanced up at him, he thought her complexion looked a little green. But he dismissed the notion. The fluorescent lights, combined with the shadows of the underground garage, cast an unnatural glow on everything. Walking around to the driver's side, he opened the door and slid behind the wheel. "I know a great little place not far from here."

She looked as if she intended to protest again, but when he started the car and backed from his parking spot, she clamped her mouth into a tight line, closed her eyes and leaned her head back against the seat.

Brett felt a twinge of guilt that he'd insisted they have dinner, when it was plain to see she was dead on her feet. But reason won out. She had to eat. This way she wouldn't have to worry about cooking something for herself when she went home. Satisfied that he'd be doing her a favor by taking her to dinner, he steered the car out of the garage and into the flow of traffic on Michigan Avenue.

Ten minutes later he helped her out of her coat and held the chair while she settled herself at his usual table for two in a corner of the restaurant. Removing his overcoat, Brett hung both wraps on a nearby hook, then seated himself and stared at her over the flicker of a candle stuck in a Chianti bottle. She looked thoroughly exhausted.

"Why don't we save this discussion until Monday morning?" he asked. "You look like you're ready to drop."

"I'm fine," she insisted. She extracted a notepad from her shoulder bag. "I'd like to get the preliminaries out of the way so I can get started with the interviews Monday morning. Have you been filled in on what I'll need from you, Mr. Connelly?''

Brett leaned back in his chair and folded his arms across his chest as he tried to get his mind back down to business and off of the erotic scenario her innocent question evoked. He could think of several very exciting things he'd like for Elena Delgado to ''need'' from him, but scheduling meetings with his family wasn't among them.

Clearing his throat, he focused on the job his father had assigned him, which Brett had been eager to accept. He wanted nothing more than to get to the bottom of who had tried to kill his brother Daniel. ''When Dad called, he said you wanted to interview the rest of the family to help with your investigation.''

She nodded. ''That's right. Your father told me you'd take care of setting up the times and place.''

He grinned. Being efficient and anticipating others' needs were the very reasons he was considered one of the best PR men in the textile industry. ''I've already got the jump on it. I've arranged for you to speak privately with each of them in a conference room at Connelly Tower, starting Monday.''

''Good.''

''But it may take several days to get all of them rounded up,'' he warned her.

He propped his elbow on the table and cupped his chin in his hand as he watched her brush a strand of silky brown hair from her flawless cheek. He'd have liked nothing more than to touch her soft skin, to run his hands through her hair. The dancing candlelight cast a soft glow on her lovely face, and Brett wondered what it would be like to hold Elena close, to kiss her.

"I understand that it will take several days to speak with everyone," she said, bringing him out of his delightful musings. She glanced up from making notations on the notepad. "I'd also like to interview some of the employees at Connelly corporate headquarters. They may have information that will aid my investigation."

"That can be arranged. Anything else?"

"Not that I can think of." She glanced at her notes. "Of course, I'll need to interview you, too." She gave him a half smile. "I don't see any reason why we can't take care of that this evening."

Heartened by the small gesture, he decided he might not be losing his touch after all. Although it hadn't been the warmest of expressions, it was a start and gave him something to build on.

"Not tonight," he said, shaking his head. "I'm tired and so are you. Besides, I'm your first interview Monday." He grinned. "You wouldn't want to throw off my schedule before we even get started, would you?"

She frowned. "I doubt that my taking your statement now will make a difference."

"Oh, but it would," he said, trying not to smile. "We wouldn't be able to enjoy our dinner and I might get indigestion. If I did, it would probably keep me awake tonight and I wouldn't get anything done tomorrow because of being tired. Then on Sunday I'd have to catch up on all the things I missed doing on Saturday, and…" He tried to affect a pitiful expression. "Well, I think you see how it would throw off my schedule."

She stared at him for several long seconds before she slowly placed her pen on the table. "Let's get something straight right now, Mr. Connelly. This isn't a social—"

Their waiter chose that moment to place a basket of bread sticks on the table. "Good evening, Mr. Connelly. Would you like a wine list?"

When Brett gave her a questioning look, Elena shook her head and smiled up at the man. "No wine for me."

"A glass of wine will help you relax and take the edge off the day," Brett said. Turning to the waiter, he added, "Bring two goblets and a bottle of your best wine, Vinnie."

Elena did a slow burn. Brett obviously had the idea that because he was extraordinarily handsome, very successful and a member of the influential Connelly family, he could control any situation he pleased. Boy, oh boy, was he in for a rude awakening.

Any other woman would probably be down on her hands and knees, thanking the moon and stars that she was dining with the very eligible Brett Connelly. But Elena wasn't just any woman. Fortunately for her, she was immune to his movie star good looks, his bluer-than-blue eyes and his engaging smile. She'd been down that path before and learned her lesson well. The last thing she wanted to have to deal with was a playboy like her ex-husband.

She started to tell their waiter not to bother bringing a glass for her, but Brett chose that moment to speak to the young man hovering beside him. "And I think we'll both have a salad with the house dressing and the calamari, Vinnie."

"Very good choice, sir," Vinnie said, treating

Elena to a grin that said he'd watched Brett in action before.

As soon as the waiter walked away, Elena glared at Brett. "Don't you think that was a bit presumptuous of you?"

"You don't like calamari?" he asked, looking shocked. "I thought everyone liked it. If you'd prefer I order something else—"

When he raised his hand to hail Vinnie, she shook her head. "That's not the point, Mr. Connelly."

With a recalcitrant lock of wavy black hair hanging low on his forehead and confusion written all over his handsome face, he looked like a little boy who had no idea what he'd done wrong. She almost smiled. She'd bet he didn't wear that expression very often.

"What is the point, Elena?" He placed his hand on hers where it rested on the top of the table. "And please, call me Brett."

All thoughts of him looking like an innocent little boy were instantly erased. His warm palm caused the oddest sensation to course through her, and his rich, smooth baritone was releasing a herd of butterflies in her less-than-stable stomach. She quickly snatched her hand away and placed it in her lap. The man deserved every bit of the playboy reputation reported in the society columns. Too bad he was wasting all that charm on her. Thanks to her ex-husband, Michael, she was totally immune to that kind of tactic.

"I told you I didn't want wine," she said. The fluttering in her stomach changed to a churning sensation, and her palms turned cold and clammy. "I think it's time we set some ground rules, Mr. Connelly. I'm not interested in anything but the investigation of your brother's attempted murder, so you can stop this right here and now.''

One dark brow rose in question as he stared at her. ''What makes you think I'm trying to do anything but cooperate with your investigation, Elena?''

''Mr. Connelly—''

''Call me Brett.''

''You steamrolled me into having dinner with you.'' She gathered her notepad and pen and jammed them into her shoulder bag. ''*You* decided I could wait to interview you until Monday, then you even went so far as to decide that I'd have wine when I clearly stated that I didn't want it. Do you see a pattern here, Mr. Connelly?''

''Not really,'' he said, mesmerizing her with his guileless blue eyes and sexy-as-sin voice.

''I don't like being told what to do,'' she said, needing to put some distance between herself and Brett Connelly. She quickly rose to her feet, but the room swayed and she had to place her hand on the table to steady herself. ''I'm used to being in control and calling the shots when I'm assigned to…an investigation.''

''Are you all right?'' he asked, jumping to his feet. To his credit, he looked genuinely concerned.

''I'm…fine.'' Elena closed her eyes in an effort to clear her vision. When she opened them again, Brett was standing at her side with his hand beneath her elbow. ''It's been a long trying day, at the end of an exhausting week, Mr. Connelly. I think I'll skip dinner, catch a cab and go home.''

''I'll drive you.''

''No, it isn't necessary,'' Elena said, trying desperately to fight the increasing dizziness. "Please, stay...and enjoy your...dinner."

Brett studied her for several long moments. He wasn't sure what the problem was, but he knew for certain Elena suffered from more than just a simple case of exhaustion. Her breathing had become shallow and labored, and her face had become a ghostly white.

"Mario," Brett called, motioning for the maître d'. When the little man hurried over to them, Brett explained, "Ms. Delgado isn't feeling well and we've decided not to have dinner after all."

"Very well, Signore Connelly," Mario said, shooting Elena a worried look as Brett held her coat. "I'm sorry the *signorina* has fallen ill. I hope she will be all right."

Nodding, Brett took her by the elbow and started to guide her toward the door. But the moment she turned, her steps faltered and she stopped abruptly. She looked up at him, and he could see a mixture of fear and panic in her expressive brown eyes, and the desperation as she sagged against him.

"Please...help me...Brett," she whispered, a moment before her lashes fluttered shut and she lost her battle with consciousness.

Without a second thought, he swung her up into his arms, cradled her to his chest and shouldered his way through the exit. Fortunately, he'd been able to park in front of Mario's and it was only a few feet to his car.

He quickly placed her on the passenger seat of the Jag, fastened her seat belt, then trotted around the front of the car to slide into the driver's seat. Jamming the key into the ignition, he shifted into first and shot from the parking space.

"Hang on, Elena," he said, fighting an unfamiliar sense of panic as he wove his way around slower-moving vehicles. "I'll have you in Memorial's E.R. in less than two minutes."

Two

Brett loosened his tie, jammed his hands into the front pockets of his suit pants and paced outside of the examining room at Memorial Hospital's E.R. He was used to having women fall at his feet figuratively, but this was the first time it had ever happened literally. And the worst part of it was, he was to blame.

How could he have pulled such a stupid stunt? Elena had told him she didn't want to go to dinner, that she'd had a bad day and just wanted to go home. But he couldn't take no for an answer.

No, Brett Connelly, connoisseur of women, had taken her reluctance to spend time with him as provocation for turning on the charm—as if she was a challenge to be conquered. He'd noticed several times that she looked as if she wasn't feeling well, but he'd ignored it. He'd even gone so far as to convince himself that a little wining and dining was just what Elena needed to improve her mood. How could he have been so insensitive, so damned stupid?

"Brett Connelly, you're the last person I expected to see here," a female voice called.

He looked up to find Meg O'Reilly walking toward him. Great. What else could go wrong this evening? Not only was he responsible for a woman collapsing at dinner, now his past was coming back to haunt him.

Brett hadn't seen Meg in five years, not since the night the pretty blonde had told him she loved him and intended to marry him as soon as she finished medical school. It had only been a month after his twin brother, Drew's, wife, Talia, had died and the devastation his brother suffered had been too fresh in Brett's mind. As with most twins he'd felt Drew's pain almost as if it was his own. Brett had made a vow never to put himself in the position to experience that degree of guilt, of failure.

So he'd taken Meg home that evening and kindly, but firmly, explained to her that he wasn't the marrying kind. He'd tried to assure her that although there wasn't any possibility of a long-term relationship, they could still see each other. But she'd taken exception to his honesty and ended up throwing a lamp at him as he'd made a hasty escape.

Now, spotting in her hand some clear plastic tubing used for IV feedings, he figured she'd probably use it to lynch him right in the hospital corridor.

"Hello, Meg," he said cautiously. As a matter of habit, his gaze zeroed in on the ring finger of her left hand. Relief coursed through him at the sight of her shiny gold wedding band. "How have you been?"

She pointed to the M.D. after her name on the white lab coat she wore. "I finally made it through medical school." She gave him a wry grin. "And I see you're still checking out women's ring fingers."

Brett nodded absently. His mind had already returned to the petite police detective in the room across the corridor. It seemed as if she'd been in there for hours.

"Could you do me a favor, Meg? Could you check on a patient and find out what's going on?" he asked suddenly, pointing to the closed door in front of them.

"Sure." She glanced toward the crowded waiting area. "Is the patient a family member?"

He shook his head. "No. It's a woman I was having dinner with. She fainted."

Giving him a contemplative look, Meg turned toward the door he'd indicated. "I'll find out what I can."

He waited for what seemed an eternity before the door finally opened. "Is she going to be all right?" he asked, his guilt increasing as he faced Meg. Her expression gave nothing away and only served to heighten his anxiety.

If he'd caused whatever Elena had been suffering from earlier in the evening to worsen by insisting she go to dinner with him he'd never forgive himself.

"As long as she takes it easy she should be fine." Meg smiled knowingly. "They're getting ready to release her as soon as the attending physician prescribes medication for the nausea. But your job is going to be to see that she starts eating regular meals and getting more rest. It's important for everyone, but even more so for someone in Ms. Delgado's condition."

"Okay." He'd agree to anything, if it would make up for his colossal lack of sensitivity.

Meg's expression turned serious. "If she doesn't, she'll lose the baby, Brett."

"The baby," he repeated dumbly.

"Yes, the baby." Meg's beeper went off, and after checking the tiny screen, she smiled. "I've got to run." She touched his arm, her face filled with understanding. "Look, Brett, she's very upset and scared to death that she'll have a miscarriage. I can tell she and the baby mean a lot to you. Just take good care of them and everything should be fine."

"Me?" Brett opened and closed his mouth several times in an attempt to make his vocal chords work. "I didn't— I mean, I'm not—"

"Relax. You'll be a great father." Meg turned to walk away. "Good luck to the three of you."

Astounded, Brett watched the woman disappear around a corner, then looked at the closed door in front of him. Meg thought Elena's baby was his.

The assumption that he was the father was almost laughable. For that matter it held true of his being the father of anyone's baby.

He shook his head as he waited for Elena. If the truth came out, most of the society gossips would be shocked right down to the soles of their feet. Brett Connelly might have been seen dining or attending a social function with several different women, but he hadn't been seeing anyone steadily for the past six months. And beside being extremely careful to take the proper precautions when he was with a woman, it had been more than a year since he'd had sex.

Fear clawed at every fiber of Elena's being, and tears blurred her vision as she slowly got dressed. One thought kept running through her mind. She couldn't lose this baby. She just couldn't. Having already suffered two miscarriages during her disastrous marriage, this was her last hope for a child of her own.

She took a deep breath and forced herself to think positively. In seven months she'd have a beautiful child to love who would love her in return. This time she was *not* going to lose her baby.

Wiping the tears from her cheeks, she hoped with all her heart that Brett had gotten tired of waiting and left the hospital to pursue other interests for the evening. She took pride in her job and had worked very hard to earn her position as a special investigative detective. When she was on duty, as she had been this evening, she never allowed anyone to see her as anything but a consummate professional. Ever.

But Brett had witnessed her weakness, her vulnerability. It would be humiliating enough to face him on Monday morning when she began interviewing the Connelly family. Tonight it would be downright impossible.

Tucking the prescription and blister packs of medication the doctor had given her for nausea into her shoulder bag, she pushed open the door of the tiny examining room and walked out into the hall. She almost groaned out loud. There Brett stood looking as tall and handsome as ever.

He whirled around at the sound of her footsteps, and the look on his face surprised her. She would have expected a sullen impatience about him for the inconvenience she'd caused. Her ex-husband, Michael, had always worn that look whenever she'd done something to interrupt his plans. But Brett's expression held nothing but concern.

"Are you all right?" he asked, closing the space

between them to place his hands on her shoulders. She found the warmth from his palms oddly reassuring.

She nodded but couldn't meet his worried gaze. How could she? She was far too embarrassed. He'd witnessed her at one of the lowest moments of her life.

"Is there someone I should call?" he asked. "A husband or friend?"

Still unable to meet his gaze, she shook her head. "There's no one."

Placing his forefinger under her chin, he lifted her face until their gazes met. "I'm really sorry, Elena," he said, his voice soft and low. "I should have listened to you when you said you weren't up to having dinner with me. Do you think you can find it in your heart to forgive me for being an insensitive fool?"

His gentle touch, the sincerity in his words and the apologetic look he gave her caused tears to flood her eyes again and a huge lump to form in her throat. She couldn't remember the last time she'd heard a man apologize to her for anything, let alone ask for her forgiveness. In the entire four years of her marriage, Michael had only expressed regret a couple of times and he'd *never* asked for her forgiveness. Not the first time, when she'd discovered he was having an affair. Not the last time, when he'd told her he was moving out to live with the woman he'd been sleeping with for the previous six months of their marriage.

"Thank you for your help," she said, forcing words past the tightness clogging her throat. "But you shouldn't have waited. I'm sure you have more entertaining things to do with your evening than stand around the hospital."

"No problem," he said, smiling. He held her coat for her. "When we get to your place, I'll call and have some food delivered."

Elena shook her head. "Thank you, but you don't have to do that. I'll catch a cab and fix something for myself when I get back to my apartment."

"The doctor said you needed to start eating regular meals and getting more rest." Brett ushered her toward the exit at the end of the long corridor. "You can't possibly do that if you have to cook for yourself. Besides, it's late and you're tired. You need to put your feet up and take it easy."

"I'm used to fending for myself," she argued. Tears were threatening again, and she had to get away from him before she humiliated herself further with a crying binge.

"It's the least I can do. I feel responsible for you spending your evening in the E.R."

As they walked out into the bitterly cold night, he put his arm around her shoulders and tucked her to his side to shield her from the brisk wind blowing in from Lake Michigan and the snow that had begun to fall. Before she could find her voice to tell him that he owed her nothing, he had her settled in the plush leather passenger seat of the Jaguar and was sliding into the driver's seat.

"Do you think your stomach would be okay with soup?" he asked.

"I think so, but you don't have to—"

"Elena, I *do* have to," he interrupted. "I should have listened to you. But I didn't, and my lack of sensitivity put you and your baby in danger. I'm really sorry, and I want to make it up to you. Please allow me to do that."

That did it. The combination of his heartfelt apology, the self-reproach reflected in his blue eyes and her unstable hormones touched something deep inside of Elena that she'd thought long dead. Her eyes flooded with tears, and she quickly turned away before he noticed.

But it was too late. He had noticed.

He immediately pulled her into his arms. "Elena, honey, please don't cry." Brett held her close and caressed her cheek with his hand while she sobbed. "Everything is going to be all right. You and the baby will be just fine. The doctor told me that you need more rest, and I'm going to make sure you get it."

Her tears fell faster. Great! Not only was she crying because of her pregnancy hormones, she was also shedding tears of utter humiliation that he'd witnessed her collapse at the restaurant and her teary breakdown now.

His warm embrace, the feel of his arms tightening around her to draw her to his wide chest, almost made her believe he meant what he said. Almost. But having been married to a man just like Brett, she knew better. Men would say anything to get themselves off the hook or to manipulate a woman into doing what they wanted.

But at the moment she was too tired and emotionally drained to protest. All she wanted was to go home, crawl into bed and forget this day had ever happened.

When she finally felt in control enough to speak, she gave him the address of her apartment building. "Please, just take me home."

Nodding, he released her, started the car and shifted

it into gear. "That's not far from here. I'll have you home in no time."

Brett looked around as he pulled the Jag to a stop behind a waiting cab in front of a shabby four-story building. Although it was a respectable middle-class neighborhood, it was clear to see that her landlord hadn't seen fit to keep his property maintained.

"Thank you for the ride home, Mr. Connelly."

Brett's brow rose at the formal use of his name and the hand she offered for him to shake. So she was trying to turn back time and return to a business-only acquaintance.

Well, that was just too damned bad, he decided, ignoring her gesture. He'd spent a good two hours in the E.R. worrying about her, and that, in his opinion, took them well beyond a business association.

Besides, whether she admitted it or not, she was extremely fragile right now. She needed someone to be there for her, to lend her moral support. And since he was partly to blame for her problems this evening, Brett felt obligated to see that she was comfortably settled before he bade her good-night. The fact that he liked the way she felt in his arms had no bearing on his decision at all.

Getting out of the car, he opened the passenger door before she could do it herself. He'd told her that he'd make sure everything was fine for her and her baby, and he had every intention of carrying through on his promise.

"Mr. Connelly—"

"Brett." He smiled down at her. "I think we're well past the formalities, Elena. Now, let's get you inside where it's warm."

The cold February wind whipped the falling snow into their faces, and he placed his arm around her to hold her close. He told himself that it was just to keep her warm, to shield her from the frigid wind. But her small body pressed against his felt wonderful and he couldn't help but wonder how it would feel without the cumbersome layers of their coats.

As they reached the steps to Elena's building, a rotund lady in her fifties carrying a gym bag and resembling Nanook of the North, opened the door. "You'll have to find somewhere else to spend the night, Elena," she said, through the wool scarf covering her mouth and nose. "The furnace won't be fixed until tomorrow at the earliest and maybe not until sometime Monday. The super said it depended on when the parts he had to order got here."

Having made her announcement, Nanook hurried to the cab waiting by the curb, threw the gym bag inside, then hurled herself in after it.

"Wonderful," Elena muttered as they watched the cab drive away. "The perfect ending to a perfect day."

Brett held the door for her. "No problem. You can throw some clothes in an overnight case and stay at my place. I've got a nice large guest room and I guarantee it's warm."

He surprised himself with the invitation, but the more he thought about it, the more it made sense. Not only was it the decent thing to do, since he was partially responsible for her collapse, it was something his parents would expect of him, considering the circumstances. This woman was in charge of investigating the attempted assassination of his brother Daniel, the new king of Altaria. Brett had been assigned the task of assisting her in whatever way was needed. By having Elena stay at his place, he could follow through on his promise to see that she was all right, and if she felt like it later, they could go over the questions she intended to ask during the interviews with his family.

"No, I can't stay at your place," she said, entering the lobby of the building.

She turned to face him, and if the look on her pretty face was any indication, hell would freeze over before she agreed to his offer. Brett almost laughed. With the temperature hovering around zero, it wouldn't surprise him to hear that it had already started icing up.

"Don't be ridiculous, Elena. You and I both know you can't stay here."

"I'll…I'll stay at…"

When her voice trailed off, he nodded. "That's what I thought. You don't have any idea where to stay, do you?"

"I'll check into a hotel," she said stubbornly.

He shook his head. "That's not acceptable."

She treated him to an indignant look. "Oh, really? And why not?"

"Because you need someone to take care of you."

He immediately wished he'd used a little more diplomacy and phrased his statement differently. He could tell by the sudden straightening of her slender shoulders and the sparks of anger in her wide brown eyes, that he'd made a huge blunder.

"Mr. Connelly, I have never nor will I ever need someone to take care of me. I've been by myself for as long as I can remember and I've done just fine. I see no reason why that should change now."

He told himself he should just walk away, that she

didn't want his help. But whether she wanted it or not, it was clear she needed it. He had no idea where the man was who'd gotten her pregnant, but it appeared as if he was out of the picture and she was on her own. For some reason that bothered him more than it should.

Brett didn't fully understand what he was about to do, or why, but he'd made her and her unborn child a promise. It was time to play his trump card. "Elena, you don't want to lose your baby because of some misguided belief that you'll relinquish your independence. Think of what's best for your child. If that means staying at my place tonight, then swallow your pride and accept my offer."

Her expression instantly changed from fiercely indignant to anxious and frightened. He felt like an absolute jerk.

Reaching out, he drew her into his arms. "I'm sorry. I shouldn't have said that."

Elena nodded her head. "Yes, you should. You're right. I should be thinking how this will affect the baby. But it would be best if I went…"

Where would she go if not to a hotel? She certainly couldn't go to a relative's. She didn't have any. Her last foster mother—the only person who had cared enough to try to get close to her, and who'd made an effort to stay in touch after Elena left the foster care system—would be more than happy to help her. But Marie Waters lived over three hundred miles downstate in the tiny little town of Johnston City. No help there. She could go to a friend's house, but she really hadn't become close to anyone since her divorce last year. And it seemed that Michael had won custody of the few friends they'd made during their turbulent marriage.

As Brett continued to hold her, she felt her resolve to refuse his offer start to melt. They were really no more than strangers, yet he was offering to take her into his home.

A warmth began to steal into her soul that she hadn't felt in a long, long time. She tried to ignore it. She didn't want to think of Brett Connelly as anything more than a shallow self-centered playboy like her ex-husband. It was the only way she could keep things in perspective and maintain their professional relationship.

He rubbed his hands up and down her back in a soothing manner as he held her close. "Can't think of anyone to stay with?"

She reluctantly shook her head. "Not really."

He held her a moment longer, then set her away from him. "It's settled, then." He gave her one of his charming smiles, blew on his hands, then rubbed them together. "Now, let's go upstairs to your apartment, throw some things in a bag and get going. It's freezing in here."

Three

Twenty minutes later Brett parked his car in his assigned space in the basement garage of his building and escorted Elena to the elevator. It was all she could do to keep from groaning when he punched in the security code to open the door. What was it with Brett and elevators, anyway? Why couldn't he live and work on the ground level? Or at the very least, take the stairs up to his condo?

She held her breath and said a silent prayer that the medication the E.R. doctor had given her had had time to take effect as the door swished open and they stepped inside. To her immense relief, the ride wasn't nearly as upsetting as she'd feared it might be, and when they stepped out into the hall on the twelfth floor, her stomach was only mildly queasy.

Brett guided her to the far end of the building where the more expensive penthouses were located, unlocked and opened the door. "Don't be surprised if the place is a wreck," he warned her. "Babe destroys something every time I'm late coming home from work."

"Babe?" He was living with someone?

He nodded and turned on the light in the foyer just in time for Elena to see a small ball of long black hair come racing around the corner. The little dog yipped and bounced around happily at her feet, but when Brett bent down to pick up the animal, it skittered out of his reach, turned around and glared at him.

"So that's the way it's going to be, huh?" He laughed and guided Elena into the spacious living room. "She'll be ultrafriendly with you, but I'll get the cold shoulder for the rest of the evening."

When he turned on the lamp by the end of the couch, he let loose a muttered curse. "Well, it looks like I'll be shopping for throw pillows again."

Elena couldn't help but laugh as she looked around at the stuffing strewn across the thick beige carpet. "I take it you've been down this path before?"

Nodding, he helped her out of her coat. "Every time I'm late coming home from work."

"She only does this when you're late? What about during the day?" Elena asked, bending down to pick up a hunter-green satin remnant and several chunks of stuffing.

"Don't do that," he said, sounding alarmed. He motioned toward a comfortable-looking, overstuffed brown armchair with a matching ottoman. "Sit down and put your feet up while I get this cleaned up."

"I'll help."

"No, you won't." He took the destroyed fabric

from her and led her to the chair he'd indicated. "Just sit back and take it easy. I got off lucky. She only took out two of the pillows this time. Normally she tears up three or four, then shreds a magazine or two for good measure."

Elena barely had time to settle herself in the chair before the little dog jumped into her lap. Two black eyes peered up at her from beneath a tuft of black hair a moment before the friendly animal pushed her head under Elena's hand to be petted.

"What breed is she?" Elena asked, rubbing Babe's small head.

He shrugged as he bent to collect chunks of stuffing. "The vet said she's mostly Shih-Tzu with maybe a little Pekingese mixed in somewhere a generation or two back." Straightening, he grinned. "But I'm pretty sure she has a bit of Tasmanian devil in her too."

Cuddling the furry little body, Elena smiled. "Whatever she is, she's adorable. How old is she?"

"The vet estimated she was about six months old when I found her wandering around outside of Connelly Tower. She was starving, scared of her shadow and extremely grateful." He laughed. "That was a little more than a year ago. Now she's well fed, arrogant as hell and thinks she owns me, instead of the other way around."

He left the room to dispose of the tattered pillows. When he returned a few minutes later carrying a leash, Elena noticed that he'd changed into jeans and a sweatshirt. "I hope you like Chinese food." When she nodded, he looked relieved. "Good. I just called in an order for chicken noodle soup, rice and stir-fried vegetables. It should be here in about twenty minutes.''

He walked over to snap the leash onto Babe's collar. His hand brushed hers as he fastened the snap, and heat streaked up her arm. Elena quickly pulled back.

She wasn't sure why, but every time Brett touched her—no matter how brief the contact—warm tingles radiated from the spot. ''Do you have someone to take her out while you're at work?'' she asked, hoping he hadn't noticed her breathless tone.

Nodding, he lifted the dog from her lap and set it on the floor. ''I have a dog-walking service that comes by twice a day.'' He looked down at Babe. ''Ready to go out?''

Elena laughed when the dog glanced up at him, then aloofly turned her head and, ignoring him, started for the door. ''You weren't joking when you said she'd give you the cold shoulder, were you?''

The long-suffering look on his handsome face was ruined by the grin he couldn't quite hide. ''I get no respect around here. No respect at all.'' His expression turning serious, he added, ''Just sit there and relax. I'll only be a few minutes.''

After he pulled on his coat and allowed Babe to lead him out the door, Elena propped her feet on the ottoman and thought about the many complexities of Brett Connelly. Her first impression of him had been that he was exactly like her hedonistic ex-husband. A man who lived for the moment and ran from anything that interfered with his good time or required that he take on any kind of responsibility.

She shook her head. Normally she could gauge someone's personality with complete accuracy within the first five minutes of talking to them. She had to. It was her job to assess people and decide whether they were as they appeared.

But she had to admit she might have been a bit hasty with her first impression of Brett. Not only had he shocked her with his heartfelt apology in the E.R. and later at her apartment, he'd proven his compassion and generosity by insisting that she stay at his place while the furnace in her building was being repaired.

Elena looked around at his condo, at the expensive furniture and original paintings. What self-respecting playboy rescued stray dogs then good-naturedly allowed them to destroy his things as if it were nothing more than a minor annoyance? Or promised to help a pregnant cop with no one to turn to and nowhere else to go?

When Babe jumped onto the middle of his stomach and started doing a tap dance, Brett opened one eye. "Don't tell me you have to go out now," he muttered. "It's barely daylight."

In answer, the little dog yipped, scampered up his chest and licked his cheek.

He scratched behind her ears. "Oh, so with one doggy kiss I'm supposed to forgive and forget the way you treated me last night?"

Babe curled up on his bare chest, rested her head on her front paws and stared at him with two guileless black eyes as she whined an apology.

He groaned. "Okay, you're forgiven. I'll take you for a walk. Just don't start with the sad puppy eyes."

Brett plucked the little dog from his chest, rolled to the side of the bed and placed her on the floor. As he pulled on his sweat suit, Babe danced impatiently at his feet. He just hoped she didn't start barking to hurry him along. Elena was in the bedroom just across the hall, and he didn't want to wake her. She needed rest.

He quickly tied his running shoes, picked up Babe and walked out into the hall. The door to the guest room was still closed, and he didn't hear sounds of Elena moving around. Good. They hadn't disturbed her.

Last evening, when he and Babe had returned from their walk, he'd found Elena curled up in the chair where he'd left her. He smiled, remembering the scene.

She'd looked so relaxed, sleeping like a baby, that he hadn't had the heart to wake her. She probably wouldn't be happy with him, but after he'd moved her overnight case to the guest room, he'd picked her up and carried her to bed. So sound asleep, she'd barely stirred when he'd removed her shoes and pulled the comforter over her.

But he'd been left with two very distinct impressions from having her small body pressed to his chest. The first was how soft and feminine she'd felt, and the second was how shocked he'd been by the degree of heat that had coursed through him. His body stirred at the memory, and his pithy curse made Babe turn around to give him a curious look.

Forcing himself to focus on his other impression of Elena's body, he frowned. He didn't have any experience with pregnant women, but he was pretty sure they were supposed to be a little sturdier than Elena. He'd been disturbed by how light she was and how fragile she'd felt in his arms. She couldn't weigh much more than a hundred pounds.

The doctor's orders had been for her to start eating more regular meals, and it bothered him that she'd missed dinner last night. But he would see that she made up for it this morning. As soon as he returned to the condo, he would prepare a big breakfast and make sure she ate every bite.

Half an hour later Brett opened the door of his condo to the scrumptious smell of bacon frying. "Elena?"

"In here," she called.

He quickly shed his coat and unsnapped the leash from Babe's collar. "What the hell do you think you're doing?" he demanded, walking into the kitchen. "You're supposed to be taking it easy."

"Good morning to you, too," she said, removing several strips of crisp bacon from the skillet. She looked around his feet. "Where's Babe?"

Brett jerked his thumb in the direction of the living room. "Burrowed under what's left of the pillows on the couch." He noticed that Elena had showered and changed into jeans and a gray sweatshirt with Chicago Police Academy silk-screened across the front.

"Why did she do that?" she asked, removing a carton of eggs from the refrigerator.

"She always does that to warm up after she's been out." He took the carton from Elena and placed it on the counter.

"I don't blame her," she said, smiling. "February in Chicago can be miserably cold." She reached for an egg. "How do you like your eggs? Sunny-side up, over easy or scrambled?"

"Over easy." He took the spatula from her hand

and guided her to the table in the breakfast nook. "But I'll take care of it. You sit down."

"I'm perfectly capable of cooking." Her eyes narrowed. "Just as I would have been capable of putting myself to bed last night if someone had bothered to wake me."

He'd figured on her having something to say about that. "You were tired."

"That's beside the point," she said stubbornly.

"No, Elena. That *is* the point."

He watched the color heighten on her cheeks as the sparkle of anger grew in her beautiful brown eyes. Propping his fists on his hips, Brett glared down at her from his much taller height. He hated using intimidation with anyone, and especially with a woman. But if it kept her from overdoing things, he'd do whatever it took.

"You're supposed to take it easy, and I'm going to make sure you do," he said sternly. "Besides, you're my guest. So sit down."

She glared at him as if she intended to argue further, then finally relented and seated herself at the table. "Brett, I..."

To his horror her eyes filled with tears and her perfect lips trembled. His gut twisted into a tight knot. He hadn't thought her feelings would be hurt over something as trivial as his insistence that she relax, while he finished cooking breakfast.

"Elena, honey, I'm sorry," he said, kneeling in front of her. He took her hands in his. "Please don't cry."

"I hate this," she said, pulling away. She covered her face and cried harder.

He felt like a world-class jerk as he wrapped his

arms around her and pulled her to him. "I don't blame you for hating me, honey. I was out of line. I shouldn't have spoken so harshly."

She shook her head and sobbed into his shoulder. "It's not you. It's me."

"You?"

She nodded and Brett had no idea what she meant. But at the moment he didn't care. Her small body pressed to his, the feel of her arms wrapped around him and her warm breath teasing the sensitive skin of his neck were wreaking havoc with his good intentions.

"It's...hormonal," she sobbed. "I can't...control it."

So that was it. Her uncontrollable crying was due to her pregnancy.

Thinking back several years, Brett remembered his twin brother, Drew, mentioning that his wife had experienced all kinds of emotions while she was pregnant with their daughter, Amanda. In fact, he and Drew had jokingly referred to Talia's sudden mood swings as the Nine-Month Nutsies.

Of course, they hadn't dared mention that to Talia or any other woman. They'd had better sense than that.

"Feeling better?" he asked when Elena's sobs tapered off and her shoulders stopped shaking.

She nodded and pushed away from his embrace. "I'm so embarrassed," she said, her voice nothing more than a whisper as she stared down at her clasped hands.

He retrieved a handful of tissues from the box on the counter, then gently touched her damp cheek to wipe away her tears. "Don't be embarrassed. It goes along with being pregnant."

Elena looked up at him with one perfect brow raised questioningly. "You've had experience with pregnant women before?"

"No, but my twin brother's late wife had a lot of trouble with her emotions when she was pregnant," Brett explained. "That was back when Drew and I still confided in each other."

The look on his handsome face, the sadness in his deep baritone made Elena wonder what had happened. "You're no longer close?"

"Not as close as we were." He shrugged, but she could tell it still bothered him. "After Talia died, Drew pretty much shut himself off emotionally from the rest of the family."

"Why did he do that?" she asked, unable to understand why anyone would distance themselves from their family at the very time they needed them most. If she'd ever had a family, she knew for certain she would have turned to them innumerable times for their love and support. It would have made coping with her two miscarriages and the breakup of her marriage so much easier.

Brett stood and walked over to the stove. He broke a couple of eggs into the skillet before he spoke again. "I think Drew pulled back from the family emotionally because he blames himself for Talia's death. She died of a drug overdose when their daughter was little." Brett turned to face her. "The rest of the family knew there was something wrong with her, that she was taking way too much prescription medication, and we tried to tell him. But Drew was in denial about her problems. When he finally found the evidence and faced facts that his society bride was addicted to drugs, it was too late. He came home from work one day to find her dead.''

''I remember reading about that. That must have been awful for him.''

He nodded. ''And the media just added to it. Since she was a Van Dorn, married to a Connelly, the newspapers were like sharks in a feeding frenzy. Every publication from here to Milwaukee carried the story, and most of the television and radio stations gave it more than average attention.''

Having dealt with reporters at crime scenes, she was well aware of the tactics used by some reporters to slant the facts or to create a story where none existed. But when two of Chicago's most prominent families were touched by the same scandal, it was noteworthy. Factor in Brett's mother, Emma, being the former princess of Altaria and it would naturally become front-page news.

''There are times I've despised dealing with the media,'' Elena said sympathetically. ''More than once they've complicated and, at times, even jeopardized investigations.''

''That doesn't surprise me.'' Brett removed two plates from the cabinet and scooped the eggs onto them. Turning back to the stove, he broke an egg into a bowl, beat it, then poured it into another, smaller skillet. ''How long have you been a policewoman?'' he asked.

''I've worked for the Chicago P.D. ever since I left the foster care system eight years ago—first as a file clerk in records, then as soon as I turned twenty-one, I applied and was accepted into the academy.'' She frowned. "Are you expecting someone else for break-fast?"

"Nope." Grinning, he shrugged. "I like over easy, but Babe prefers her egg scrambled."

Elena smiled back at him. "I've been meaning to ask, why did you name her 'Babe'?"

A flush rose on his lean cheeks. "I, uh, don't think you'll care much for my answer."

"Try me."

He cleared his throat, then took a deep breath. "Not long after I found her, I discovered that women were drawn to cute little dogs."

"Oh, please. Tell me you didn't."

Nodding, the color on his cheeks deepened. "Her full name is Babe Magnet."

Brett placed the last plate in the dishwasher, then walked into the living room to find Elena curled up on the couch with Babe. He watched Elena dig into her shoulder bag and extract her notepad. She scribbled something on the top page before looking up at him.

"Would you mind my asking you a few questions about your family?" she asked.

"I'd rather wait until Monday, if you don't mind."

She gave him a suspicious look. "Why? Don't you want whoever made the attempt on your brother's life caught immediately?"

"Don't get me wrong. I want the S.O.B. caught as soon as possible. But not at the expense of your health." He sat down beside her. "Daniel is safe now, and I'd rather wait until Monday when you've had more rest."

"I'm fine," she said, her cheeks coloring a pretty pink.

He knew she was still embarrassed that he'd witnessed her collapse and the crying jags. She viewed it as weakness and a loss of control—something he was quickly learning that she found intolerable.

"The doctor said—"

"Oh, brother." She rolled her eyes. "Will you get over that? You sound like a broken record."

"I told you I'd make sure you took it easy and didn't overdo." He removed the notepad from her hands and placed it on the coffee table.

She glared at him a moment before she reached out and picked it up again. "Don't worry about it, Connelly. Sitting here on my buns isn't all that taxing."

He pried the paper from her fingers and tossed it into the chair across from them. "What are your regular days off?"

The sound of her throaty laughter sent a streak of heat straight up his spine. "There's no such thing as a set schedule with regular days off for an SIU detective," she explained. "If we're assigned to an investigation, we may be off duty, but we're always on call."

"Always?" He didn't like the sound of that at all.

"Day and night," she said, nodding.

She rose to her feet to retrieve the notepad, but when he caught her hand to stop her, she stumbled and wound up on his lap. They stared at each other for several long seconds before he finally spoke. "Why don't you give me a break here, Delgado?" He ran his index finger down the soft skin of her cheek. "I'm trying to keep my promise to see that you take it easy."

A myriad of emotions flashed in her chocolate brown eyes, but the strongest, most identifiable was awareness. Satisfaction and male pride coursed through him. So, the lady wasn't as immune to him as she'd tried to let on.

"You have no idea how beautiful you are, do you?" he asked, tracing the perfect cupid's bow of her upper lip with the tip of his finger.

"I've never given it much thought."

"Why not, Elena?" He watched her tongue dart out to moisten the spot he'd just touched.

She shrugged. "Probably because I don't care."

Brett was astounded. He'd never met a woman quite like her. Most of the women he knew were overly concerned with their beauty, some of them to the point of obsession. But he could tell that it truly didn't matter to Elena. Amazing.

The pager in her shoulder bag suddenly went off, causing her to jerk away from him. "You're off duty," he reminded her. "Ignore it."

"I told you, I'm on call," she said, scrambling from his lap. She pulled the offending beeper and a cell phone from her purse, glanced at the tiny screen, then started to make a call. "Rats! The battery on my phone is dead. May I use yours?"

Brett stared at her for endless seconds before he finally nodded and pointed toward the kitchen. "I left the cordless unit on the counter by the coffeemaker."

Two hours after he'd taken Elena home, Brett and Babe took turns prowling the condo like a pair of caged tigers. The page Elena had answered had been from one of her neighbors, advising her that the furnace had been repaired and that it was warm enough

in their building for her to go home. He'd tried to talk
her into staying for another night, but she'd insisted
that she would rest better at her own apartment. He'd
finally given up and driven her home.

He looked around the living room and couldn't believe how empty and abandoned it felt. Which, he
decided, was completely ridiculous.

He'd lived alone since college and preferred it that
way. While some of his friends had shared apartments
after graduation, Brett had moved into his own place.
He liked living alone, and until last night he hadn't
even had a woman spend the entire night with him in
the six years he'd lived there.

Brett stared out at Belmont Harbor as he tried to
figure out why he felt the way he did. It wasn't like
he and Elena had shared great sex, or anything beyond companionable conversation. He could better
understand his wanting to be with her if they had.
And although he certainly wouldn't object to their
making love, it wasn't foremost on his mind.

He swallowed hard. He'd never in his life had the
hots for a pregnant woman and he wasn't at all comfortable thinking about it now.

No. It was more that he felt a need to protect her.
Which, he was certain she'd be quick to tell him, was
absolutely ridiculous. She was a cop—a veteran of at
least five years experience on the streets of Chicago—
and perfectly capable of taking care of herself. Besides being an intelligent, independent woman, she
carried a gun, and he had no doubt she knew how to
use the weapon quite well. He would also lay odds
on the fact that she was *very* good at her job. She
wouldn't have been promoted to the position of an
SIU detective if she wasn't. And even though the

thought of her facing a meaner-than-hell criminal made anger and apprehension burn at his gut, it wasn't physical harm that he wanted to shelter her from.

He'd recognized a vulnerability about her that she valiantly tried, but couldn't quite hide. At least not from him. He'd glimpsed a flash of deep loneliness in her eyes last night at the hospital when she'd told him there was no one to call. Then he'd seen it again at her apartment when she'd reluctantly admitted there was nowhere she could go for the night.

Coming from a large, loving family, he couldn't imagine not having their emotional support. But she'd mentioned being a child of the foster care system, and it seemed she had no one to turn to for help of any kind. And that bothered him. A lot.

He left the floor-to-ceiling window at the end of his living room to pace into the kitchen. He met Babe coming out as he walked in.

"It's not right for anyone to be *that* alone," he told the little mutt.

In answer, Babe's plume of a tail drooped and she let loose a low, mournful whine.

Brett nodded. "My sentiments exactly."

Four

Tucking a strand of hair behind her ear, Elena tried to concentrate on what Drew Connelly was saying. The man looked exactly like Brett, which was distracting enough. But to her dismay she found herself comparing the differences between the two men—their personalities, their mannerisms.

She'd always heard that with a set of twins, one tended to be an extrovert and the other more introverted. And that certainly seemed to hold true with the Connelly brothers. Brett was the outgoing charmer, while Drew seemed to be more serious and withdrawn. Of course, Brett had told her Drew changed after the tragic death of his young wife. That might have something to do with the differences between the two men.

Without warning, the door to the conference room suddenly opened and Brett strolled into the room as if he had every right to be there. Elena wasn't the least bit surprised. He'd had an excuse for interrupting every interview she'd conducted so far. Why would this one be any different?

"What is it this time, Mr. Connelly?" she asked, allowing her impatience to color her tone.

"Just checking to see if things are going well." He flashed her an unrepentant grin—the same one she was quickly coming to realize always made her insides tingle and her heart skip a beat.

"Everything was fine until about ten seconds ago," she answered wryly.

Elena tried to ignore the way his blue oxford cloth shirt hugged his wide shoulders and complemented his deep-azure eyes. Or how an errant lock of his raven hair, hanging low on his forehead, made him look like a mischievous little boy.

But there was nothing childlike about the look he was sending her way. It felt as if he caressed her with his eyes. She swallowed hard and tried to ignore the heat warmimg her. She didn't want or need a man in her life.

"I think you're making a nuisance of yourself, little brother," Drew said, a ghost of a smile playing at the corners of his mouth.

"You think so?" Brett asked, laughing. "I guess because you're fifteen minutes older than me, you think you're a lot wiser?"

Drew nodded. "Wise enough to see that you're annoying Detective Delgado."

Elena watched the exchange with interest, relieved that Brett had turned his attention to his twin and from her. She'd never had a sibling—never had anyone— with whom to share the same type of easy banter. A twinge of loneliness tightened her chest and she quickly turned her attention to her notes, away from all that she'd missed in life.

"Is there anything else you need from me, Ms. Delgado?" Drew asked, glancing at his watch. He rose from his seat at the conference table. "My daughter is home from school today with a cold and I need to call the nanny to see how she's feeling."

Elena shook her head. "No. I think we've covered everything."

Drew hadn't been present when the attempt was made on his brother's life and, therefore, was unable to add anything pertinent to the investigation. And his answers had been consistent with what Brett had told her over the weekend. Drew's wife, Talia, had died several years ago of a prescription drug overdose, leaving him with a young daughter.

At first, Elena had followed procedure and treated his recount of his wife's death as if there might be a connection. But after reviewing the facts, she determined that the two cases were completely unrelated. With his inheritance of the Altarian throne, Daniel had become the target of an assassin, while Talia had been the unfortunate victim of her own indulgence and self-destructive lifestyle.

Elena smiled. "If I have more questions, I'll contact you."

"Be sure you do," Drew said, nodding. "I'd like to see the person responsible for trying to kill Daniel caught and put away for good."

"We're doing our best to accomplish just that," Elena assured him, standing to shake his hand. "Thank you for your time, Mr. Connelly. I hope your daughter is feeling better soon."

Drew nodded, then walked to the door. Turning back, he pointed to his twin. "A word of advice, Brett," he said, his eyes twinkling with humor. "You'd better stop being your usual pesky self."

"What makes you say that?" Brett asked, innocently. "I'm just trying to be helpful."

"You're forgetting that the lady carries a gun," Drew answered. "She just might decide to use it on you if you don't leave her alone and let her do her job."

When Drew closed the door behind him, Elena turned her attention on Brett. "I also have the power to arrest you for hindering an investigation. Which I'll do in a heartbeat, if you don't stop interrupting my interviews."

Brett walked over to where she stood at the head of the big mahogany table. "Why would you want to arrest me, when all I'm trying to do is look out for your welfare?" he asked, his voice sounding so sensual that her toes curled.

He was too darned sexy for her peace of mind and way too close for comfort. What on earth was he up to?

"Mr. Connelly—"

"Brett."

"All right, Brett," she said, emphasizing his name. She pushed against his chest to back him away. She might as well have been trying to move a brick wall. The man was as solid as a chunk of granite. "There's a code of conduct concerning fraternization with—"

"Am I the victim of a crime you're investigating?" he interrupted.

"No. But—"

She pushed against him again, but this time she'd

used more force and stumbled backward when he remained immovable. He placed his arms around her waist to keep her from falling, and his nearness made her heart skip a beat.

"Am I a suspect?" he asked, resting his forehead against hers.

"N-no." He drew her even closer, aligning her body with his. How was she supposed to concentrate with him so close, with his lips hovering only a fraction of an inch above hers?

"Then it sounds to me like I'm exempt from these rules you're so concerned with," he said, his mouth brushing hers. "Correct?"

She nodded, then shook her head as she tried to make her suddenly fuzzy brain work. "It...it's a gray area."

"No, Elena," he murmured against her lips. "It couldn't be more clear."

A split second later his lips settled gently on hers, and Elena immediately forgot all about following rules or why she'd vowed over a year ago to steer clear of men, and especially ones like Brett Connelly. She didn't even give a second thought to where they were or that someone could walk into the conference room at any moment. All she could think of was how wonderful Brett's mouth felt moving over hers, how his arms were pulling her closer to his strong, muscular body.

Reason faded as Brett used his tongue to coax her to open for him, wordlessly asking for access to the sensitive recesses within. She didn't even hesitate. When she allowed him entry, he deepened the kiss, slipping inside to stroke, tease and taste her with a tenderness that took her breath away. A groan of pleasure rumbled up from deep in his chest, causing her legs to turn to rubber.

When she clutched at his shirt for support, he pulled her more firmly against him, allowing her to feel his arousal, the desire he wasn't even trying to hide. A coil of need pooled deep in her lower belly, and her sensitive breasts tingled, the nipples hardening as heat shot through every fiber of her being.

She'd been kissed before, but never like this. Never with such mastery. Not even in the early days of her marriage, when love was new and the fire of passion burned bright, had she experienced sensations so intense that she lost control of her ability to think clearly.

The sound of the conference room door opening, a quiet gasp, then the swish as it was quickly pulled shut, brought her back to her senses. What on earth was she doing? She was on duty.

Pushing against Brett's chest, she tore her mouth from his. "St-stop."

Brett allowed her to put space between them, but continued to hold her. "That was incredible," he said, his breathing labored. "You're so damned sweet. So—"

"Incredibly stupid," she finished for him. She backed away from his embrace, but Brett caught her hands in his to keep her from getting away. "I'm not interested in becoming involved with you or anyone else," she said, wishing she'd sounded more adamant.

He gazed at her for several long seconds before he spoke. "I won't deny that I liked kissing you, and that I'm going to kiss you again. But next time we'll find somewhere more private."

"There won't be a next time," she said emphatically.

His sudden grin surprised her. "Oh, there'll be a next time, sweet Elena. But only when you're ready for it."

She moved away from him and sat down in the leather chair at the conference table. She had to. Otherwise she might have fallen on the floor from the way his sexy voice made her knees wobble.

"Don't hold your breath waiting for it, Connelly." She took a deep breath. "I'm not interested in you or any other man. Period."

Brett bent down, placed his hands on the arms of the chair and leaned forward, bringing them nose to nose. "I don't know who the guy was, or what he did to hurt you, but I'm not that man, Elena." He lifted his hand to caress her cheek. "I know we could be good together. But I don't want you to feel pressured. It's not good for you or the baby."

He brushed her lips with his, then straightening to his full height, turned and left the conference room.

"This isn't good," she muttered. "Not at all."

Reaching for her appointment book, her hand shook so badly she could barely read the schedule. She breathed a sigh of relief when she discovered she'd be able to call it an early day. As soon as she spoke with the head of the accounting department, she'd go home, put her feet up and concentrate on forgetting that kiss. She didn't want to remember how it made her feel, or that it made her want things that she knew in her heart she'd never have.

Brett propped his feet on the corner of his desk, crossed his ankles, then absently checked his watch as he went through the motions of listening to his team make their report and outline what they had planned for the rest of the week. His mind wasn't on the projected reaction to the upcoming ad campaign or the latest stats concerning customer satisfaction.

One thought dominated his mind, distracting him with its disturbing implications. Nothing in his experience with women could have prepared him for the way he'd felt when he kissed Elena. From the moment their lips met, it seemed as if the world came to a screeching halt and that nothing would ever be the same again.

Now more than ever he had the overwhelming desire to get to know her better, to kiss her again and…more.

Brett suddenly had to force himself to breathe. If that didn't raise a red flag the size of Vermont in his obviously demented brain, nothing would. He didn't want to become involved in a relationship.

A sliver of panic skipped up his spine. He wasn't even comfortable with the *R* word popping into his thoughts. To him it represented being responsible for another's happiness, placing his own happiness into a woman's hands and risking the possibility of one of them failing. And *failure* was the one word Brett never allowed to enter his vocabulary. Ever.

Brought out of his disturbing introspection by the buzz of his intercom, he frowned. He'd told Fiona to hold all calls during the meeting.

"What is it, Fiona?" he asked, irritated.

"I'm sorry to bother you, Mr. Connelly," his secretary said, sounding nonplussed. "But you told me to let you know when Detective Delgado finished for the day."

Brett's feet hit the floor with a thud as he straightened in the chair. "Thank you, Fiona." To the three men and one woman sitting in front of his desk, giving him curious looks, he apologized, "I'm sorry, but we'll have to delay going over the rest of these figures until tomorrow."

Frowning, Henry Sadowski held up a folder. "But what about the—"

"It can wait," Brett said firmly. He watched the four exchange looks, then stand and silently file out of his office.

He barely had enough patience to wait for them to close the door before he pressed the page button on his intercom. "Fiona, please come in here."

When the woman entered the room, he motioned her over to the desk. "I'm sorry for being short with you, Fiona. I was a bit…preoccupied."

"It's all right, Mr. Connelly. Was there something else you needed?"

Nodding, he smiled. "Could you go down to the conference room and tell Ms. Delgado that I'll be ready to leave in a few minutes?"

"Detective Delgado has already left."

In the process of clearing his desk, he snapped his briefcase shut, then glared at his unflappable secretary. "When did she leave?" he demanded.

"I'm not sure," Fiona said calmly. "I took a late lunch. When I returned, she'd left a note on my desk saying she'd be here again tomorrow."

Frustrated, Brett barely managed to keep his oath to himself. Crossing the room, he jerked his overcoat from the coat tree. Had Elena overdone it with too many interviews and become ill? Was she experiencing problems like she'd had the other night at the restaurant?

"I'm leaving for the day," he said, stuffing his arms into his coat sleeves. He walked to the door, then turned back suddenly. He really did owe the woman an apology for being so abrupt. "Have the switchboard forward my calls to voice mail and take the rest of the afternoon off with pay."

Nodding, Fiona smiled. "Thank you, Mr. Connelly. I'll do that. Have a nice evening."

Heading for the elevators, he slowed his pace. He knew exactly why Elena had left early, and it had nothing to do with her overworking herself or feeling ill. He'd seen the apprehension, the wariness in her beautiful brown eyes right after he'd kissed her. She was putting distance between them, running from him.

And if he was smart, he'd take off in the opposite direction himself. Hadn't he spent the past half hour reminding himself of all the reasons he didn't want to become involved with Elena, or any other woman?

When the elevator doors finally opened, he walked inside and pressed the button for the parking garage. It would probably be wise to take a step back from the situation and put distance between them.

Deciding that it would be best for all concerned, he stepped off the elevator and slowly walked to his car. Throwing his briefcase into the passenger seat of the Jag, he got in behind the wheel. He'd go by her apartment later and see that she was all right, then check on her occasionally while she worked on Daniel's case. But after that, he fully intended to back off and allow her to go her way and he'd go his.

* * *

Elena covered her head with a pillow and tried to ignore the knocking on her apartment door. Maybe whoever it was would get tired and go away, then she could resume her nap.

Since the building had an intercom security lock at the entrance that required visitors to page someone inside to gain entry, the persistent person on the other side of her apartment door had to be one of her neighbors. Probably Martha McNeery again. Once she'd learned that Elena was a cop, she'd called at least twice a week to have Elena check her apartment for intruders.

"Mrs. McNeery, we've been through this before," Elena muttered, dragging herself off the couch. "There's nobody hiding in your closet, under your bed or outside on the fire escape."

Before she could get to the door, the knocking turned to pounding. "I'm coming, Mrs. McNeery," Elena shouted, shoving her feet into her slippers. She didn't know why she bothered saying anything. The woman never had her hearing aid turned up enough to hear anything unless it was loud enough to wake the dead.

Flinging the door wide, Elena opened her mouth to ask Mrs. McNeery what the problem was this time, but to her surprise she found Babe bouncing around her feet. "What are you doing here, sweetie?" she asked, bending down to scoop the little dog into her arms.

When she straightened, Brett stood in front of her, holding a large sack. "Looks like somebody just woke up," he said, his blue eyes twinkling.

Elena blinked, then glanced down at her oversize

sweatshirt, baggy sweatpants and moccasin slippers. She must look a mess.

She'd come home right after leaving Connelly Tower, changed clothes and curled up on the couch with the intention of reading through her notes. She glanced at the clock on the VCR. She'd been sleeping for the past three hours.

"Are you going to let me in, or do I have to stand out here in the hall while our dinner gets cold?" Brett asked good-naturedly.

Stepping back, she silently watched him carry the sack into the kitchen, remove his coat and start pulling out containers of food. The delicious smells of something Italian wafted throughout the room, making her suddenly ravenous.

Brett walked over to the cabinets and started opening doors as if he belonged there. He removed a couple of plates and glasses, then glanced over his shoulder. "Where do you keep the silverware?"

"Make yourself at home, Connelly," she said, closing the door.

He gave her an unrepentant grin. "Silverware?"

"First drawer on the left." She set Babe on the floor, then asked the little dog, "Is he always this pushy?"

Babe wagged her tail and yipped as if to say yes, then headed straight for the couch to burrow under the afghan.

"Don't listen to her," he said, setting the table. "Sometimes Babe exaggerates."

"I have a feeling she's telling the truth this time," Elena said dryly. She watched him move around her kitchen a moment longer before she asked, "What are you doing here, Brett? And how did you get into the building?''

''Your neighbor, Nanook of the North, was coming out as I—''

''Mrs. Simpkins,'' Elena corrected.

''Okay. Mrs. Simpkins let me in as she was leaving.'' He smiled. ''And I'm here to make sure you eat right.'' He started removing lids from the containers of food. ''By the way, Mario says hello and he's glad to hear you're feeling better.''

''Brett, you don't have to keep checking up on me.''

He ignored her and pulled a bottle from the sack. ''I figured wine is out because of the baby, but I thought sparkling grape juice would be okay.'' He held it out for her perusal. ''It is, isn't it?''

She nodded. ''Yes, but—''

''Great.'' He opened the bottle and filled the glasses he'd placed beside the plates. ''I hope you like vegetable lasagna. I thought it would be more healthy for you than regular lasagna.''

''You didn't have to do this,'' she said, wondering what she was going to do with him. He was the most infuriating and at the same time endearing man she'd ever met.

''I know I didn't have to do it.'' He grinned. ''But when I stopped by Mario's on my way home from work, I remembered that on Friday night you missed trying some of the best Italian food in Chicago. Besides, I didn't feel like eating alone.'' He grinned. ''Babe doesn't talk much during dinner.''

Elena couldn't keep from laughing. ''So you think she talks to you at other times?''

He nodded. ''Maybe not in the conventional way,

but she definitely lets me know what she's thinking and what she wants.''

"Ah, yes. I almost forgot about the throw pillows,'' Elena said, settling in the chair he held.

"Is your car out of the repair shop?'' he asked, opening another container.

"Not yet.'' Sighing she shook her head. "The mechanic said it would be sometime next week before it's fixed.''

Nodding, Brett removed several meatballs and placed them in a small bowl he'd pulled from the bag, then, setting it on the floor, he seated himself. "Come and get it,'' he called to the dog. To Elena he said, "I'll pick you up tomorrow morning.''

"That's not necessary,'' she insisted, shaking her head. "I can get there on my own.''

"Maybe so, but I'll be by around eight to pick you up.'' Before she could protest further, he pointed to her plate. "Go ahead and eat before it gets cold.''

Brett kept a close eye on Elena's plate and was satisfied that he'd done the right thing when she finished all of the lasagna. He still wasn't sure why he'd made the decision to pick up food on his way over to check on her, but he was glad that he had. It was clear she hadn't eaten since lunch.

"Thank you. That was heavenly,'' she said, when she'd finished the last of two soft breadsticks. "I'm stuffed.''

"I'm glad you liked it,'' he said, rising to take their plates to the sink. When he looked for, but couldn't find, a dishwasher, he ran water into the sink to wash the dishes.

"You don't have to clean up,'' she said, carrying

their glasses to the counter. She stood at his elbow. "I'll take care of it."

He shook his head. "Nope. You need to rest. Why don't you join Babe on the couch?"

"I can't do that. You're my guest."

She tried to shoo him away from the sink, but he wasn't about to budge. "I invited myself over for dinner, so technically, I don't think I could be considered a guest," he said, adding dishwashing liquid to the water.

"Look, Connelly, I'm not going to stand here and debate the issue." She reached for the sponge, but he held it out of her reach. "You furnished dinner. I'll take care of cleaning up."

He shot her a stubborn look. "What do you say we compromise? I'll wash and you dry?"

She gave him an odd look. "You really don't mind?"

"What gave you the idea I would?" he asked, wondering at the confused expression on her pretty face.

"Probably because Michael would have died before he offered to help." She shrugged. "And if he had, he wouldn't have meant it."

"Who's Michael?" Brett asked, careful to keep his voice casual, despite the fact that every nerve ending in his body was drawn up tighter than a violin string.

"My husband." She shook her head. "Make that my ex-husband."

Brett nearly dropped the plate he held as he connected the name. "You were married to Michael Delgado?"

Grimacing, she nodded. "Afraid so. I can't say it's the smartest thing I've ever done. Even my foster mother, Marie, thought he was a snake. And she always managed to find something good about everyone." Elena looked chagrined. "But I didn't listen to her and lived to regret it."

Brett certainly wasn't going to argue with her on that one. Michael Delgado was an assistant district attorney, reputed to be one of the biggest skirt chasers in Chicago and as slippery as an eel.

"I didn't know he'd ever been married," Brett said truthfully. "How long were you together?"

She dried the plate he handed her, then placed it on a stack in the cabinet. Just when he decided she was going to ignore his question, she answered.

"I don't think he knew he was married, either," she said, her tone reflecting her disgust. "I was married for four years, but I don't think he ever was. He never seemed to remember that little detail about himself. The ink hadn't much more than dried on the marriage license before he started going out with other women."

It suddenly occurred to Brett that the man had to be her baby's father. "How does he feel about the baby?"

Frowning, Elena asked, "It didn't seem to matter to him the two times I was pregnant with his babies. Why would he care about this one?"

Brett stared at her. "This is your third child?"

The sudden look of sadness crossing her expressive features caused his stomach to twist into a tight knot. "No, I miscarried both times," she said quietly.

Every muscle in his body tensed. He had a feeling he knew, but he had to ask. "How far along were you?"

"Two months."

Aside from the obvious reasons, it was no wonder Elena was terrified by the problems she'd been experiencing. She couldn't be more than a couple of months along with this baby. "Do the doctors know what was wrong?" he asked gently.

She shrugged. "Stress mostly. I was trying to work full-time, become a mother and hold together a marriage that never was."

"So Michael isn't the father of this baby?"

"No," she said, sounding relieved. "He walked out on Valentine's Day last year, I filed for divorce a week later and I haven't seen him since."

"Then who...?" Brett let his voice trail off, afraid she might tell him to mind his own business.

But instead of the outrage he expected, she laughed. "You're probably never going to believe this. I have no idea who the father is."

That did it. Brett did drop the second plate. Fortunately, the dishwater slowed its descent and kept the heavy ironstone from breaking on the bottom of the sink. The water splashed onto them but neither noticed.

"Don't look so shocked." She shrugged. "All I know about the father is he's six feet two inches tall, has blue eyes and black hair." Her gaze raked him from head to toe, then laughing, she added, "For all I know, he could be you."

Brett's heart slammed against his ribs so hard it felt like he might have cracked a couple. When he finally found enough breath to speak, all he could manage to get out was a strangled, "Me?"

Laughing harder, she reached out to touch him, and on contact a current coursed up his arm, then headed straight for the region below his belt.

"Relax, Connelly." Her chocolate-colored eyes twinkled with humor. "You don't have anything to worry about. Unless, of course, you've ever made a deposit at the Partners in Fertility sperm bank."

Brett shook his head. "Never even considered it."

"I didn't think so." She dried the last plate, put it in the cabinet, then closed the door. "My donor was an intern from one of the hospitals."

"Why?" Brett couldn't stop the single word from escaping.

"They pay for donations and I've heard that medical students sometimes supplement their schooling by being donors," she answered.

"No. I mean why—"

"Go to a sperm bank?" she asked. When he nodded, she explained. "It was the only logical solution. I get the baby I want, without the complications of a relationship I don't. And I won't have to share custody with anyone." She took the sponge from him to wipe off the kitchen table. "The baby will be mine alone."

Sweat popped out on Brett's forehead and upper lip as a feeling so strong it almost brought him to his knees raged through him. It quickly passed, but for a moment he'd felt a keen disappointment that Elena hadn't waited for him to father her child.

Brett suddenly felt the need to run like hell.

"I need to be going," he said, making a show of glancing at his watch. He grabbed his coat and Babe, then headed for the door. "I just remembered I have another appointment this evening."

Five

Waiting for her last morning interview to show up, Elena propped her elbow on the mahogany conference table, rested her chin on her hand and stared out of the floor-to-ceiling windows at Lake Michigan. As had been the case so many times over the past five days, Brett Connelly filled her thoughts. Since Friday evening she hadn't been able to keep her mind off him. Of course, that probably had a lot to do with the fact that he hadn't allowed her to think of much else.

She'd rarely, if ever, allowed anyone to bowl her over the way he had. And she never opened up to anyone the way she had with him last night.

It bothered her that she'd been so forthcoming with information about herself—things she normally considered nobody's business but her own. But Brett had been extremely easy to talk to and more than a little understanding.

Of course, her ex-husband had been that way in the beginning. When she'd first met Michael, he'd showered her with attention, pretended to listen to what she had to say and appeared to care about the same things that mattered to her. But all too soon she'd discovered it was nothing but a ploy, a way to learn where she was the most vulnerable and to use it to his advantage.

When they met, Michael had needed a wife in order to obtain the promotions within the district attorney's office that the family-oriented D.A. thought to be essential for his assistants. Once Michael had discovered that she'd grown up alone and desperately wanted to have a family of her own, he'd used that to entice her into marrying him. But just a matter of weeks after the wedding, the D.A. had suffered a fatal heart attack, and his replacement didn't see the need to base promotions on his assistants' marital status. So Michael Delgado had been saddled with a by-then pregnant wife, he didn't want.

Shaking off the disturbing memories, Elena checked her watch. Apparently, her eleven-o'clock interview was going to be a no-show. The man had probably gotten busy with something and couldn't break away. Understandable, considering the many duties of the executives working for a company the size of Connelly Corporation.

It was just as well, she decided, rising from her chair to walk down the hall to speak with Brett's secretary. She had a doctor's appointment right after lunch, and with her car still in the shop for repairs, she'd have to catch the L.

"Fiona, will you please call and reschedule my interview with Robert Marsh?'' Elena asked when the secretary looked up at her approach.

''Of course.'' The woman picked up the phone. ''Would you like to meet with him later this afternoon?''

Elena shook her head. ''I have a doctor's appointment and won't be conducting interviews again until tomorrow morning. Could you see if he's available sometime within the next couple of days?''

''Certainly,'' Fiona said, already dialing the man's extension.

Walking back to the conference room, Elena collected her things and had just put on her coat when Brett burst into the room. ''What's wrong?'' he demanded, rushing over to her. He placed his hands on her upper arms and eased her down into the nearest chair. ''Are you feeling dizzy? Nauseated? What? Why didn't you have Fiona page me?''

The concern on his handsome face rendered her temporarily speechless. When she finally found her voice, she shook her head. ''I'm all right. What made you think otherwise?''

''Fiona said you're on your way to the doctor.'' He released her but didn't move away. ''If you're feeling fine, why do you need to see a doctor?'' he demanded.

She couldn't believe how worried Brett looked. Her ex-husband hadn't shown that degree of concern either time she'd miscarried. She smiled reassuringly. ''I'm going to the obstetrician because I have regular prenatal checkups. Today's appointment is one of them.''

''Oh.''

Brett straightened and rubbed the tense muscles at

the base of his neck with a less-than-steady hand. He felt foolish as hell. But as soon as Fiona told him Elena was leaving to see a doctor, fear had knifed through him with an intensity that was staggering.

So much for his decision to back off and only be around her when it was an absolute necessity. "What time is your appointment?"

"One o'clock, but since Robert Marsh was unable to make it for our scheduled interview, I thought I'd take an early lunch, then go on to the doctor's office." She rose and began gathering her purse and briefcase. "I'll see you tomorrow."

He took hold of her arm when she started past him. "Wait a minute. I thought you told me last night that your car is still in the repair shop."

She nodded. "It is. And the guy called this morning to tell me he has to order another part that will probably cost me a small fortune."

"I'll drive you," Brett said, guiding her toward the door and out into the hall.

"Thank you for the offer, but I'll catch the L."

"No way," he said, steering her toward his office. "I don't like you riding the L."

She stopped to glare at him. "It doesn't really matter whether you like it or not. Back off, Connelly. It's not your call."

The thought of her riding the elevated train alone made his stomach hurt. "It's not safe."

"I think I can handle myself well enough to survive," she said dryly.

Telling himself she carried a gun, knew how to use it and probably had enough self-defense training to take down a full-grown gorilla didn't alleviate Brett's concerns. He didn't like having to use the trump card again, but dammit the woman was as stubborn as anyone he'd ever met.

"Given your past history of miscarriages, I doubt the excitement would be good for you or the baby in the event that someone tried to accost you."

He hated the haunted look that flashed in her big brown eyes, the worry lines that suddenly creased her forehead. But she had to see reason.

"That was a low blow, Connelly," she said, her voice nothing more than a whisper. "You're not playing fair."

Brett felt like the biggest jerk in the tri-state area, but sometimes the woman let that independent streak of hers override common sense. "I'm sorry, Elena," he said, pulling her into his arms. "But you have to think of the baby."

Conscious that they were standing in front of Fiona's desk and that the woman was openly gaping at the scene in front of her, Brett led Elena into his office. Once the door was closed behind them, he framed her face with his hands. "I know you've been trained to take care of yourself, but the circumstances are different now. It's not just you anymore. It's Peanut, too."

"Who is Peanut?"

"The baby." He had to make her understand. "You have to consider the potential risks these things pose for him, too."

"Her," she said, frowning. "You know, Connelly, I really hate when you're right."

"I do, too, honey."

He lightly kissed her forehead, then set her away from him. If he hadn't put distance between them, he wasn't sure he could stop himself from taking her into his arms and kissing her until they both collapsed from a lack of oxygen.

"Let me cancel my meeting for this afternoon," he said, walking over to his desk. "We'll stop for something to eat, then I'll drive you to your doctor's appointment."

"You don't have to do that," she said, shaking her head. "You stay here and take care of whatever you need to do. I'll get a cab."

He snorted. "That's not much better than the L. The last thing you need is to be in a car accident."

She glared at him. "You don't drive any better than cabbies. You zip that Jag in and out of traffic like you're jockeying for position in the Grand Prix."

He laughed. "Yes, but I know what I'm doing."

"And you think they don't?" she asked incredulously. "Oh, brother! You've got an ego that just won't quit."

Grinning, he nodded. "And you know what they say about the male ego."

"What would that be?" she asked, one perfect brow rising in question.

"It's fragile," he said simply.

That got a good laugh out of her. "Where did you hear that?"

"All the talk shows have devoted at least one program to the topic, and the women's magazine are constantly printing articles about how to do this or that without shattering a man's ego," he answered as he collected a stack of papers to shove into his briefcase.

"You read a lot of those, do you?"

Smiling at the laughter he detected in her voice, he shook his head. "Not in this lifetime. But I have sisters who read them."

He pressed the button on his intercom, quickly instructed Fiona to reschedule his appointments for the afternoon, then shrugged into his coat and took Elena by the elbow. "Where's your doctor's office?"

When she gave him the address, he grinned. "I know this great little mom and pop joint not far from there. They have the best cheddar-baked potato soup in the city."

An hour later, as they drove away from the little Irish pub, Elena had to agree with Brett about the soup. Served in sour dough bread bowls, it was delicious and without a doubt the best she'd ever eaten.

"How are the interviews coming along?" he asked, steering the Jag into the flow of traffic.

"Everything is progressing nicely." She settled back in the leather seat. "I've interviewed all of your brothers and sisters, except for Seth."

"Seth had to be in court this week," Brett said, downshifting the powerful car in order to make a turn. "He should be available by Friday. If not, he'll definitely be freed up by the first of next week."

"Isn't he the attorney?" She couldn't help but wonder what it would be like to have so many siblings, or what it would be like trying not to confuse what they did for a living. "Are you close?"

"We weren't when he first came to live with us," Brett said, weaving the Jag through the midday traffic. "Back then Seth was too angry to become close to anyone. But in the last few years I'd say we've become pretty good friends."

Elena frowned. "I'm confused. If Seth didn't live with your parents, where—"

"Seth is my half brother," Brett interrupted. He

looked straight ahead, but she could tell he was deciding just how much he should tell her. Finally, as if coming to a decision, he shrugged. "You might as well know, my parents separated for a time right after my brother Rafe was born. That was thirty-three years ago. Seth's mother, Angie Donahue, was Dad's secretary at the time."

Elena noticed that Brett's hands tightened on the steering wheel. "Let me guess. She was more than ready to console him?"

Brett nodded. "After Mom and Dad got back together, Angie quit Connelly Corporation and dropped out of sight. Dad made sure that he provided support for Seth, but apparently the woman didn't have a clue about raising kids. By the time Seth was twelve, he was so out of control, she packed him up and signed over custody to my dad."

"That must have been a very difficult time for all of you," Elena said. Having been in foster homes with troubled youths, she was well aware of the disruption one angry child could cause a family.

"Drew and I were only seven at the time, but I can still remember a lot of it." Brett turned into the parking garage of her obstetrician's office building. "It didn't take long for Mom and Dad to see that if they didn't do something pretty quick, Seth was headed for big trouble. Dad checked around to see where he could get Seth the best possible help, then pulled some strings to get him admitted into one of the best military schools in the country. That's where Seth straightened up his act."

"He's lucky they found the right place for him," Elena said, remembering several children from her past who weren't as fortunate. "Does he see his biological mother very often?"

Brett got out of the car and came around to open the passenger door. "Nobody's seen Angie Donahue since the night she dropped Seth off on our doorstep."

"That's odd," Elena said thoughtfully. "Why wouldn't she want to at least check on Seth from time to time?"

"You'll have to ask her about that," Brett said, guiding her into the covered walkway bridging the garage and the office building. "If you can find her."

"I think it might be a good idea if I check on her whereabouts just to be on the safe side," Elena said as they rode the elevator to the third floor.

When they stepped out into a waiting room, Brett removed his coat and found them a place to sit while Elena registered with the receptionist. He was more than a little surprised to see that he wasn't the only man in the waiting area. He had no idea why the others would be there, unless they'd come along to lend moral support for someone like he'd done for Elena.

"They should be calling me in just a few minutes," Elena said, handing him a magazine. "I thought you might like something to read while you wait. I'm sorry, but they don't seem to have a big selection, and this was about all that was left."

He read the title aloud. *"Pregnancy and Birth."*

Laughing, she removed her coat. "It was either that or a pamphlet titled, Your Uterus and You."

He chuckled. "I don't think I have much need for that."

"I didn't think so, either." She hesitated, then

asked, "Would you mind watching my coat while I'm in seeing the doctor?"

"No problem," he said, taking it from her and placing it across the empty chair on the other side of him.

"Elena Delgado," a nurse called at the doorway of several long corridors branching off from the waiting area.

"I shouldn't be long," Elena said, following the woman.

Settling back in the chair, Brett had just opened the magazine when the same nurse walked up to him. "Are you with Ms. Delgado?"

"Yes. Is something wrong?" He was halfway out of the chair when her smile stopped him.

"No, everything's fine," the woman assured him. "I just thought you might want to be with Ms. Delgado. This is something I don't think you'll want to miss."

"Okay," he said, confused. He wasn't sure what the woman wanted him to see, and he was positive Elena wouldn't like his being there, but curiosity had him rising to his feet. Collecting their coats, he followed the nurse down the corridor Elena had gone down only minutes before.

When he opened the door to the room the nurse indicated, he found Elena lying flat on a examining table, staring at the ceiling. She turned her head at the sound of his entrance, and her friendly expression vanished immediately.

"What are *you* doing here?" she demanded. She obviously wasn't of the same opinion as the nurse about his not missing whatever was about to take place.

"I was told I'd want to see this," he explained, noticing that she'd changed into a hospital gown. The fact that she probably didn't have on a stitch of clothing beneath the ugly garment sent his blood pressure up several points.

She glared at him as she pulled at the sheet that draped her from the waist down. "Trust me, you don't. Now get out."

He ignored her protest and walked over to the examining table. "Don't get upset. It's not good for you or the baby."

"This isn't any of your concern, Connelly."

Tossing their coats over the chair at the side of the table, he placed his hands on her shoulders to keep her from rising to a sitting position. "Calm down."

"No."

Her cheeks had colored a pretty pink, and her brown eyes glittered with anger. He didn't think he'd ever seen a woman look more beautiful.

Brett wasn't sure why it had suddenly become important to him that he witness whatever mystery event was about to take place, but it had. Knowing only one way to silence her adamant protests, he leaned down and firmly placed his lips over hers.

At first Elena pushed against his chest with her hands, but as he moved his mouth over hers, he felt her relax a moment before she slipped her arms around his neck. Primitive male satisfaction filled him at her acceptance, and he forgot all about where they were or the reason for the kiss.

When her lips parted on a sigh, Brett seized the opportunity and slipped his tongue inside. Her tiny moan of pleasure encouraged him and he boldly explored her soft mouth, tasted the sweetness that was

Elena. The tentative touch of her tongue to his sent heat coursing through his veins and made his heart thump hard against his rib cage.

Lifting her to a sitting position, he wrapped his arms around her and slid his hand into the split at the back of her gown. The silky feel of her skin beneath his palm made breathing difficult and his arousal not only predictable but inevitable. He wanted her, and he could tell by her response that she wanted him.

The door opened suddenly, reminding him that he'd once again forgotten his vow to restrict their contact to business only. Lightly brushing his lips over Elena's one last time, he loosened his hold and laid her back onto the examining table.

When he turned, a woman in a white lab coat smiled as she pulled a folder out of a pocket on the door. "Good afternoon, I'm Dr. Simmons."

He shook the hand she extended. "Brett Connelly."

"I see you had a few problems this past weekend," the doctor said, turning her attention to an uncharacteristically quiet Elena.

Sensing that she needed the support, Brett took her hand in his.

"Besides the usual nausea, I've had some problems with dizziness," Elena answered.

"She fainted Friday evening," he added.

Brett felt her hand flex in his, and he gently returned the pressure, lending her his strength. He glanced at her to gauge how she was holding up, and his heart twisted at the vulnerable look on her pretty face.

"I've spoken with the staff at Memorial and they've filled me in on the details," Dr. Simmons said, reviewing the chart. Snapping the folder shut, she smiled. "I don't think we have anything to worry about, but I want you to continue to get plenty of rest and eat well-balanced meals."

"Okay," Elena said, her voice reflecting how relieved she was at the news.

"Is there anything else she should do or avoid doing?" Brett asked, drawing a stormy look from Elena. He ignored it as he waited for the doctor's answer.

"Given Elena's history of miscarriages, I wouldn't advise her running a marathon or lifting anything over ten pounds," Dr. Simmons said. Apparently thinking that he and Elena had an intimate relationship, she smiled. "But I see no reason to avoid less strenuous activities, including lovemaking."

Elena shook her head. "We haven't—"

"I'm sure the doctor understands, honey," Brett interrupted, barely able to keep a straight face.

Dr. Simmons nodded. "You should be able to enjoy normal relations until a month or so before delivery." She grinned. "Now, what do you say we take your baby's first picture?"

Brett wasn't sure what the woman meant, but it seemed to please Elena immensely. He'd never seen her look this excited and happy.

"Can we tell anything at this point?" she asked.

"It's a possibility. You're close enough to your third month that we may be able to see something," Dr. Simmons said, pulling down the sheet to just below Elena's waist and pulling the bottom of the gown up to expose her gently rounded stomach.

Fascinated, Brett watched the doctor squeeze a generous amount of a clear lubricant just below Elena's navel, then remove what looked like a microphone from the side of a monitor to press it into the thin gel. She moved it around in a circular pattern on Elena's lower abdomen until a fuzzy picture popped up on the monitor.

"There's your baby, Elena," Dr. Simmons said, grinning.

He watched tears fill Elena's eyes. "Oh, she's beautiful," she whispered, her lips trembling.

"It's a girl?" he asked, staring intently at the screen. "How can you tell? I don't see anything that even resembles a baby."

"It's a little too early to determine the sex," Dr. Simmons answered. "I think Elena's hoping for a girl." She pointed to the screen. "See, there's an arm and a leg."

What the hell did they see that he didn't? All he could decipher from the fuzzy black and gray image was that something in the middle of it twitched rhythmically. Then, as if by magic, the picture cleared. Or maybe he'd concentrated on it long enough to understand what Elena and Dr. Simmons had seen all along. He wasn't sure, but Brett suddenly felt as if the breath had been knocked out of him. A tiny hand, complete with a thumb and four fingers, became discernible as it moved on the screen.

"My God! That's awesome." Without a second thought he leaned down and kissed Elena with all the awe and wonder that the moment held for him.

Tears of happiness slid silently from the corners of Elena's eyes as Brett's lips moved gently over hers. When he lifted his head, he smiled down at her. "Thank you for allowing me to see this, Elena."

"Thank you for being here with me," she whispered, surprised that she really was happy to have him there to share the moment.

She'd never made it far enough in her other two pregnancies to have a sonogram, to see the tiny life within her. But she knew that if she had, her ex-husband wouldn't have bothered to make it to the doctor's office for the first look at their child. The only interest Michael had had in the miracles they'd created together had been how it would affect his career or cramp his style. Beyond that, he simply hadn't cared whether they had a baby or how much of an emotional toll losing it had taken on her.

As she gazed up at Brett, she wondered how she could have come to the conclusion that he and Michael were cut from the same cloth. In the past week Brett had shown more concern and offered more in the way of moral support than Michael had in the entire four years of their marriage. And not once had Brett complained about being inconvenienced in any way.

"Here's your baby's first portrait," Dr. Simmons said, handing Elena a printed copy of the sonogram.

"Would you make another copy of that?" Brett asked.

Clearly amused, Dr. Simmons smiled. "Of course."

She quickly made adjustments, and the machine spit out another picture. "Now, do you have any questions or complaints that I should know about before we do the rest of the examination?"

Elena thought for a moment. "I don't think so. I'm taking my vitamins, and with the medication the nausea is bearable."

"I'm making sure she doesn't overwork herself,"

Brett volunteered. He sat down in the chair beside the table as if he intended to stay.

"Could you excuse us a moment, Dr. Simmons?" Elena asked.

Dr. Simmons nodded. "I'll be back in a few minutes. I have to get a couple of brochures to give you."

"Thank you," Elena said as the woman quietly closed the door behind her. Turning her head to look at Brett, she tried to keep from laughing. He obviously didn't have a clue what was going to happen next. For some reason she found that fact quite endearing. "I think you'll be more comfortable out in the waiting room, Brett."

"Don't worry about me," he said, staring at the picture of the sonogram. "I'm fine."

"This isn't about you. I'm more worried about *my* comfort level." When his head snapped up, she almost laughed at his confused expression. "The doctor is going to be doing a routine examination on other parts than just my stomach."

His brows shot up as understanding dawned. "Ohh…one of those." Rising to his feet, he gathered their coats and walked to the door. "I'll, uh, be in the waiting room if you need me."

Brett sat with his forearms propped on his knees, staring at the picture he held in his hands. He was completely unaware of the other occupants in the waiting area. One thing kept running through his mind—he'd never in his life felt more humbled or privileged than when the image of Elena's baby had popped up on the sonogram screen. And although she hadn't invited him to witness the first glimpse of the child growing within her, Elena had been easily persuaded to allow him to stay.

He sat back in the chair and thought about the apprehension he'd seen in her expressive brown eyes, the fear, when the doctor had first walked into the room. Whether she admitted it or not, Elena needed someone to be with her, to hold her hand and lend her emotional support.

Brett leaned his head back against the wall and stared at the ceiling. So much for his decision of keeping his distance from her, he thought, feeling more than a little uneasy. To his dismay he was quickly discovering he wanted to be the one she turned to. And that scared the hell out of him.

For the first time in his life, he wanted to be needed, wanted to take care of someone other than himself. And that was where the problem arose. He wasn't sure he could do that without giving more of himself than he was willing to invest.

Six

When Brett arrived at Connelly Tower the next morning, he was furious and itching for a fight. Bypassing his office, he walked straight into the conference room. He found Elena there, nibbling on a bagel as if she didn't have a care in the world.

"I went by your apartment to pick you up this morning." He removed his overcoat and threw it at one of the chairs, not caring if it hit the mark. "Imagine my surprise to find you'd already left."

Glancing up at him, she smiled. "I'll bet that was a surprise."

"Did you get your car out of the repair shop?"

She scribbled something on the notepad in front of her, then finished the last of the bagel before she answered. "Nope."

"How did you get to work this morning, Elena?" he asked, trying to stay calm despite the churning in his stomach. He dreaded to hear what he knew she was going to say.

"I took the L."

"I thought we discussed the dangers of you taking the train alone," he said, careful to keep his tone even. What he really wanted to do was shout that she'd taken an unnecessary risk and in the process scared the living hell out of him. It hadn't been until he walked into the conference room that he'd known for sure she was all right.

When she looked up at him, she shrugged. "You discussed it. I didn't."

"But you agreed—"

"No. I didn't agree to anything." She slowly placed her pencil on the table, then rose to her feet. "You told me about all the dangers riding on the L could pose to my pregnancy. You even insisted that riding in a cab wasn't the answer." Poking his chest with her finger, she glared up at him. "Do *you* see a pattern here, Connelly?"

Elena was gaining steam as she went, and Brett didn't think he'd ever seen her look more beautiful. Reaching out, he loosely wrapped his arms around her waist. "I sure do, Delgado." He dropped a kiss on her forehead. "I see you being too stubborn to see that Chicago's transit system isn't safe for you and the baby."

"That's bull and we both know it." She sounded a lot more breathless now than angry.

Brushing her lips with his, Brett marveled at how perfect she felt in his arms even though there was a good eight-to-ten inch difference in their heights. "Elena, I don't like you using public transportation."

"Tens of thousands of people do it every day and nothing happens."

"I don't know those people," he said stubbornly.

He knew he was being unreasonable, but he didn't care. He wasn't at all comfortable with the thought of Elena alone on the train or a bus. And it didn't make him feel any better to think of her taking a cab ride with the driver weaving in and out of traffic at breakneck speeds on the overly crowded Chicago streets.

"Then how do you suggest I get to work, or anywhere else, for that matter?" she asked.

He rested his forehead on hers. "I'll drive you."

"I can't ask you to do that."

"You're not asking," he said, placing a kiss on the tip of her nose. "I'm volunteering."

Lowering his mouth to hers, he reveled in the feel of her perfect lips beneath his, the softness that was uniquely Elena's. When she slipped her arms from between them, he expected her to push him away, but to his satisfaction, she encircled his neck, welcoming his embrace.

Encouraged by her gesture of acceptance, he deepened the kiss to reacquaint himself with the sweet taste of her. At the first tentative touch of her tongue meeting his, heat shot through every fiber of his being and his body responded with a tightening that made him light-headed.

He slid his hands down her back to pull her into the cradle of his hips, to allow her to feel his hardness, to let her know what she did to him. But her breasts against his chest, her tiny moan of pleasure, caused his insides to feel as if they'd been set on fire and the only way to extinguish the flames would be to make love to her.

His throbbing body reminded him of just how long it had been since he'd been with a woman. He tried to tell himself that was the reason for his immediate reaction and that thinking about making love to Elena wasn't going to help calm his libido. But he had a feeling the intensity of his arousal had very little to do with his lack of sex in the past year and more to do with the woman he held.

Kissing Elena was quickly becoming an addiction—a habit he wasn't sure he'd ever be able to break—and one he wasn't sure he ever wanted to. In that moment he knew beyond a shadow of a doubt that he was getting in way over his head.

Slowly lightening the pressure of his mouth, he lifted his head to stare down at her. Her eyes had darkened to a deep, rich chocolate and the pink blush of desire colored her smooth cheeks.

Brett took a step back in order to calm his aching body. He didn't want to walk out into the reception area in a state of arousal and traumatize his straitlaced secretary.

"What's your schedule like for today?" he asked, placing his hands on Elena's shoulders to keep from drawing her to him again.

"I...have to meet with...Robert Marsh this morning," she answered, her breathing shallow.

He picked up his coat from the chair he'd thrown it over earlier. "How about after lunch?"

"I'll be going to Lake Shore Manor at two o'clock to set up an interview with your mother's secretary, Jennifer Anderson, and to give your parents an update on your brother's case."

Confident now that he could walk out into the reception area without shocking Fiona down to the roots of her bleached-blond hair, he started for the door. "Good. We'll go out for a leisurely lunch, then drive up to Mom and Dad's." When she looked as if she intended to protest, he shook his head. He wasn't about to take no for an answer. "This isn't negotiable, Delgado. Get used to it. I'm your chauffeur until your car is repaired."

After setting up the time for her interview with Jennifer Anderson, Elena found herself sitting with the Connellys in the sun room at Lake Shore Manor. Naturally they wanted an update on the case. Elena just wished she had something more to tell them.

"I've interviewed most of your children and several of the Connelly Corporation employees," Elena said, carefully placing her china teacup on the saucer. She wasn't at all comfortable handling something so elegant and obviously expensive.

Setting them on the glass surface of the coffee table in front of her, she breathed a sigh of relief. If she chipped the delicate pieces, it would no doubt cost a small fortune to replace them.

"Did you learn anything new?" Brett's mother asked, the remnants of her European accent more pronounced due to her obvious worry.

At the age of sixty, Emma Connelly was a strikingly beautiful woman with an air of elegance that only the royals possessed. But the events of the past month were beginning to take their toll. Sadness and worry marred her otherwise flawless features, and her blue eyes reflected the anxiety that still haunted her. The former princess of Altaria, Emma had not only experienced the terror of having an assassination attempt made on her eldest son, she'd also lost her father, King Thomas, and her brother, Prince Marc, in a tragic boating accident.

Elena regretted not having news to help relieve the woman's stress. "Unfortunately, Mrs. Connelly, I haven't been able to turn up anything we don't already know."

"That's not acceptable." Grant Connelly's steel-gray eyes and granite jaw indicated that he was a man used to demanding answers and having those demands met. "Someone came damned close to killing our son. We want the SOB caught."

"We all do, Dad," Brett spoke up. He left his spot by the French doors leading out to the patio to sit with Elena on the white wicker love seat. "But these things take time." He put his arm around her shoulders, causing Emma and Grant to exchange a bemused look. "Elena's been working very hard to sort through all the facts, even at a risk to her own health."

"That's not an issue here," Elena said quickly, shrugging out of his embrace.

She gave Brett a look she hoped would keep him quiet. She wasn't comfortable sharing the intimate details of her life with just anyone, nor was she happy about the speculative expressions the Connellys wore at the familiarity their son displayed toward her. Glancing at her notes to regain her composure, she tried to find a way to turn the focus of the meeting back to the investigation.

"Mr. Connelly, since your son inherited the Altarian throne, and there were no attempts made on his life prior to his being named King Thomas's successor, we've already established that the attempt on his life had to be political in nature," she said, choosing her words carefully.

She felt confident that her tact had worked when Grant nodded. "But what we don't know is why," he said, running a hand over his face.

Emma Connelly wasn't the only one feeling the strain of the recent upheaval in their lives. The chiseled lines in Grant's distinguished face had deepened with worry over the past month, and Elena would swear that his black hair carried a few more strands of white, especially at his temples.

"No, we don't know why," she agreed. "But we do know whoever pulled the trigger was a professional. He deliberately chose a public place with the express purpose of blending into the crowd after he'd carried out the hit. That tells us there's a definite reason behind the attempt and that it's not just some crackpot seizing the first opportunity that comes along. Once we figure out exactly what that reason is, it should lead us to whoever hired the gunman."

"Excuse me, Mr. Connelly," a maid said, standing poised at the entrance of the sun room. "You have a phone call."

"Tell whoever it is that I'm tied up in a meeting," Grant said dismissively.

"You're going to want to take this," the woman insisted with all the confidence of one who'd worked for the Connellys for many years. "It's that Albert Dessage fellow you hired from overseas. He said to tell you it's urgent."

Elena immediately recognized the name of the European-based P.I. the Connellys had hired to look into the case on the Altarian end of the investigation.

When Grant rose from his chair to take the call,

the maid handed him a cordless unit. "He's on line two."

"Thank you, Ruby," Grant said, taking the phone. He waited until she'd left the room before he punched a button to take the phone off hold. "What have you discovered, Dessage?" Grant demanded, dispensing with a polite greeting.

Elena watched Grant's eyes shift immediately to Emma, then a frown crease his forehead. He listened for several more seconds, before saying, "Yes, she's here. Just a moment." Holding the phone out to Elena, he said, "Dessage wants to talk to you, Ms. Delgado."

From the look on Grant Connelly's face, she had no doubt that the case had just taken a relevant turn. Taking the phone from him, she placed it to her ear. "This is Detective Delgado, Mr. Dessage."

"As we suspected to be the case, I've just received confirmation through Interpol that King Thomas and Prince Marc were murdered," Dessage said, his voice crackling into her ear. "The boat had been rigged with plastic explosives and a timing device. It was set to explode once they were several miles out in open water. They never had a chance. They were doomed from the moment they stepped on board."

"Any leads indicating who's responsible?" she asked.

"Not at this time," the man said. "But please assure the Connellys that King Daniel and his wife are safe and have the Royal Guard's protection at all times."

"I'll do that," she said, feeling Brett's reassuring hand on her shoulder.

She heard Emma's sharp gasp and glanced up to see the woman quietly sobbing into her mono-grammed linen hankie. Apparently, Grant had given her the news that her father and brother had been murdered.

"Anything else?" Elena asked Dessage.

"Yes." Dessage's voice began to cut out, forcing her total concentration on what he was saying. "Tell the Connellys that…family should be safe. The assassinations…directly related to the throne."

With a crackling pop, the connection was lost before Elena could respond.

When she turned her attention back to the Connellys, Grant was trying to comfort a grieving Emma. "Mr. Dessage said, and I have to agree, that it's almost a forgone conclusion that the attempt on your son's life is directly tied to the Altarian throne."

"What about my other sons?" Emma asked through her tears. She glanced at Brett, then pinned Elena with a beseeching look. "Are they in danger, too?"

"Don't worry about the rest of us, Mom," Brett said. "We'll be fine."

Elena nodded, carefully placing the cordless phone on the coffee table. "I have to agree, Mrs. Connelly. As long as King Daniel is safely hidden away in Altaria, I don't think we have to be concerned about the others. He's the king now, and unless something happens to him, there would be no reason for the assassin to go after your other children." She glanced at Brett, thankful that he was too far down the royal lineage to be in much of any danger. "But I would encourage them to be extremely cautious. If they do see anything suspicious or feel threatened in any way, please advise them to call the police immediately," she said, rising to leave.

"I have a security detail here at Lake Shore Manor," Grant said, "and I'll speak with the head of security at Connelly Tower about tightening things there. Would it be advisable to have the other boys placed under surveillance?''

''No, Mr. Connelly,'' Elena said honestly. ''I don't think that's necessary. But I do believe they should be on the alert, since the men of the family are the only ones eligible to inherit the throne.''

''All right.'' Grant stood to shake her hand. ''Thank you for dropping by to give us an update.''

''No problem, Mr. Connelly,'' she said, putting her arms into the coat Brett held for her.

''Brett, please be watchful,'' Emma pleaded.

''I will, Mom,'' he said, walking over to place a kiss on his mother's cheek.

Elena couldn't make any promises concerning the woman's other sons, but she could with the youngest. ''Mrs. Connelly, Brett and I have been working very closely together, setting up the interviews and coordinating the investigation of Connelly Corporation's higher level employees. Let me assure you that I've seen nothing unusual, and as long as we're working together, you have nothing to worry about. I'll personally see to Brett's safety.''

Lost in thought, Brett silently steered the Jag through the gates of Lake Shore Manor and out onto Lake Shore Drive. He wasn't sure whether to be amused or insulted by Elena's promise to his mother.

On one hand, he found the idea of a woman as petite as Elena vowing to keep him safe almost laughable. He was at least ten inches taller and outweighed her by a good seventy-five pounds. What chance would a woman of her stature have against anyone posing a threat to him?

On the other hand, his ego had taken a glancing blow. He didn't like that she might have the opinion he couldn't take care of himself or her. Did she see him as nothing more than a desk jockey with the self-defense skills of a slug?

"Before you sit there and build my statement to your mother into a personal insult, remember this," Elena said quietly. "I'm trained to observe situations and analyze any and all potential danger." She reached over and placed her hand on his leg just a few inches above his knee. On contact a shaft of heat snaked up his spine and quickly spread through the rest of his body. "I wasn't saying you couldn't protect yourself, only that I would be there to alert you if I felt there was a threat." She gave his thigh a playful pat, sending his blood pressure skyrocketing. "Besides, I carry a gun. You don't."

Startled that she'd read him correctly, he jerked his head around to look at her. "I wasn't thinking anything like that," he lied. He wasn't about to admit that her assessment had been accurate. After all, a man had his pride.

She gave him a smile that said she saw right through him. "Whatever you say, Connelly."

How did she do that? How did she know what he was thinking? Was he that transparent?

Deciding it was time to change the subject before he opened his mouth and proved her right, he asked, "What have you got planned for this evening?"

She removed her hand from his leg and placed it in her lap. He reached over, took hold of it and placed it back on his thigh, then covered it with his own. He liked having her touch him.

"I really don't have anything planned besides a hot

bath, putting on my sweats and moccasins and vegging out in front of the TV with a toasted cheese sandwich and a can of soup,'' she answered, her voice sounding a little shaky.

Satisfied that he got to her as much as she did him, he grinned. ''Why don't we go by my condo so I can change clothes and get Babe, then we can pick up something more nutritious than soup and veg out together?''

She gave him a long look and for several seconds he thought she was going to turn his idea down. ''I have to warn you, I don't have a remote control to my TV,'' she finally said, grinning.

''My God, woman, this is the twenty-first century, not the Stone Age.'' Relieved, he gave an exaggerated shake of his head. ''A TV without a remote? What's the world coming to?''

She laughed. ''It had one, but I lost it when I moved after the divorce last year.''

''Okay, that's more like it.'' He turned off Lake Shore Drive and, driving several blocks to the west, pulled to a stop in front of an electronics store in a strip mall.

''What are we stopping here for?''

''Two words—universal remote.''

She laughed. ''You're kidding, right?''

''Nope.'' He grinned as he prepared to get out of the car. ''A man has to have a remote in his hand if he's going to do this right. It's a huge part of the vegging process.''

Three hours later Brett sat on the couch with his arm around Elena. She leaned against him while Babe snoozed lazily in her lap.

After ten minutes of watching the most mindless

show he'd ever had the misfortune to tune into, he picked up the remote he'd purchased. "This is the biggest waste of film I've ever seen," he said, channel surfing for something more interesting.

"That's what vegging is all about," Elena said, sounding sleepy. "It's sitting on the couch, watching television shows that don't inform you of something or make you think about anything."

When he paused on one of the network news programs, she shook her head. "If you don't mind, I'd rather not watch this."

"Why not?" he asked. The anchor had just announced a special report on Valentine's Day rituals around the world.

She sat up straight. "I don't much care for this particular holiday."

As Brett sat there wondering what her reasons were, understanding suddenly dawned. How could he have forgotten? A few days ago she'd told him about her husband leaving her.

"Don't think about what happened last year," he said, tightening his arm around her. "I'm sure you have more pleasant memories of other Valentine's Days."

"Not really." She placed Babe on the couch and rose to her feet. Gathering their empty popcorn bowl and soda cans, she walked into the kitchen.

Brett followed her. "You haven't had one memorable Valentine's Day?"

She gave him a wry smile as she placed the bowls on the counter. "Last year was pretty memorable."

"I don't mean that and you know it," he said, walking up to stand in front of her. "What about the years before? Didn't Delgado buy you flowers or at least take you out for dinner?''

"No," she said, shaking her head. "The closest thing I ever got from him that could even remotely be considered romantic was a call telling me we had a political fund-raiser to attend and that he wanted me to go out and buy a new dress for the occasion. That was on Valentine's Day.''

"That's it?'' Brett couldn't believe anyone was that insensitive.

Laughing, she nodded. "Then he went to a happy hour with some of his co-workers and conveniently forgot to come home to pick me up.''

"He went to the dinner without you?''

"Don't look so shocked," she said, running water into the sink to wash the few dishes they'd used. "He ended up taking his secretary to the dinner.''

Brett was outraged that the man would treat Elena so shabbily. "How long had you been married?''

"Six months." She shrugged as if it didn't matter. "I really wasn't all that surprised. By that time the honeymoon was over, and I knew exactly what I'd gotten myself into.''

"Why did you stay with him?''

Turning to face him, she smiled sadly. "Partly because I wanted our marriage to work, and partly because I didn't have anywhere else to go.''

"But—''

She placed her finger to his lips to stop him. "I didn't know right away that I'd married such a jerk," she explained. "Michael was quite good at covering up his infidelity, and I was eager to accept his excuses.''

Brett reached out to take her into his arms. "You really didn't know what was going on?''

"I knew," she admitted, resting her head against his chest. "I just didn't want to admit that I'd been so desperate to have a family that I'd made the biggest mistake of my life."

"How did you manage to stay with it for four years?" he asked, holding her close. Brett ached for the loneliness she must have felt throughout most of her life—first as a foster child and then as the wife of a philandering husband.

"It wasn't so bad." She shook her head. "Michael wasn't abusive or anything like that. For the most part we led separate lives. He went his way, and I went mine." Glancing up at Brett, her eyes begged for his understanding. "But as long as I was married, I was still part of something. I still belonged."

Brett didn't know what to say. He'd never experienced that kind of loneliness, never known what it was like not to have anyone who really loved him. He'd always been secure in the knowledge that whether it was his parents, grandparents or siblings, he belonged to someone, he meant something to.

Knowing that anything he said would be grossly inadequate, he did the only thing he could think of to convey what he was feeling—he kissed her.

Careful to keep the kiss light at first, he gently moved his mouth over hers. He wanted to let her know how much her trusting him with the secrets of her past meant to him, wanted to apologize for the inconsiderate actions of the lowest of his gender. But the feel of her breasts pressed to his chest, the electrified impulses that skipped over every nerve in his body from the tentative touch of her tongue to his lips, sent his good intentions right out the window.

Gathering her more firmly against him, he brought

his hand up to cup her breast, to tease the tip with his thumb. But the barrier of fleece between them proved to be more frustration than he was willing to put up with. Groaning, Brett slid his hand beneath the tail of her sweatshirt. Her satiny skin filling his palm and the discovery that she hadn't bothered with a bra when she changed clothes caused heat to shoot through his body with an intensity that threatened to buckle his knees.

At that moment Brett knew he wanted her more than he'd ever wanted anything in his life. And it scared the hell out of him.

Forcing himself to release her, he straightened her shirt, then stepped back. "I have to go."

Elena nodded. "I think it would be best."

"I'll be by tomorrow morning around eight to pick you up," he said, putting on his jacket.

"I won't be going to Connelly Tower tomorrow," she said, shaking her head. "I have to spend the day in my office at SIU headquarters, transcribing my notes and filing reports."

"What time should I be by to drive you over there?" he asked.

"You're off the hook for tomorrow, Connelly," she said, sounding almost relieved. "I'll be riding into work with a colleague of mine."

He stared at her for endless seconds, wondering why the thought of her not being down the hall from him tomorrow on the seventeenth floor of Connelly Tower bothered him so much. Deciding he was better off not knowing, he picked up Babe and walked out the door before he turned back and made a complete fool of himself by asking her to let him spend the night.

Seven

The next day stretched out interminably for Brett, and it was all he could do to force himself to wait until he was sure Elena had returned home from work before he called to check on her. Expecting to hear her usual clear, concise greeting, he knew as soon as she picked up the phone that something was wrong. Her voice quavered when she answered and he could tell she was sniffling back tears.

"What's happened?" he demanded, sitting up from his slouched position in the armchair. The silence on the other end of the line was killing him—second by slow, agonizing second. "Talk to me, honey. Are you all right?"

"No." Her voice was little more than a whisper when she finally answered, and he had to strain to hear her. But that one word caused icy fingers of fear to wrap around his heart and his lungs to feel as if he couldn't draw in air.

"I'll be right over," he said, punching the off button on the cordless phone. He pitched it at the couch and ran into the bedroom for his shoes. His heart pounded against his rib cage like a jungle drum and his graphic curses as he struggled into his coat sent Babe diving for cover under the couch pillows.

Driving at speeds that would probably have gotten him thrown in jail had a patrolman tried to stop him, Brett made it to Elena's in record time. Thankfully, one of the other tenants in her building was leaving as he arrived, and he dashed through the entrance without having to wait for her to buzz him in.

Taking the stairs two at a time, he ran down the hall to pound on her door. "Elena, open up!"

It seemed it took forever for her to release the locks and open the door. When she did, his heart felt as if it dropped to his feet. Tears streaked down her porcelain-pale cheeks, and her hand shook as she wiped at them with a tissue.

"What's wrong?" he demanded, pulling her into his arms. "Is it the baby?"

She shook her head as she wrapped her arms around his waist and pressed her cheek to his chest. "No."

Relieved that she still had Peanut tucked safely inside of her, he moved them farther into the apartment in order to close the door, then led her over to the couch. Sitting down, he pulled her onto his lap and held her while she sobbed against his shoulder. Unsure of what else to do, he stroked her silky brown hair and murmured what he hoped were words of comfort as her tears ran their course.

When she finally quieted, he asked, "What happened, honey?"

"I…saw Michael today at SIU headquarters." She sounded defeated.

Brett felt his gut burn at the mention of the man's name. Did she still harbor feelings for the jerk?

"And?" he prompted.

She dabbed at her eyes. "He took great delight in telling me…his new wife is scheduled for a C-section a week from today…to deliver their son."

Valentine's Day. It took a moment for Brett to remember why that day was significant. Then it hit him. It was the one-year anniversary of the man walking out on her.

Brett wasn't sure he wanted to know the answer, but he had to ask. "Does it bother you that Delgado remarried?"

"No." Her lack of hesitation made him feel a little better.

"Then what's wrong, honey?" he asked, soothing the tight muscles at the base of her neck.

She took a deep breath, then sat up to look at him. "It's ridiculous."

"That's okay," he said, giving her a smile he hoped was encouraging. "It's a big deal to you. That's all that matters."

Glancing down at her hands, she shook her head. "It just hurts that Michael's wife is able to do what I don't seem capable of doing."

"You mean have a baby?" he asked gently.

She nodded. "Why is it so easy for some women, but not me? What's wrong with me?"

"Look at me, Elena," Brett said. When she raised her eyes to meet his, he placed his hand on her stomach. "There's nothing wrong with you. You're pregnant and the doctor said you and the baby are both doing fine."

She bit her lower lip to keep it from trembling as she nodded.

"Considering the problems you had in the past, it's only natural for you to be concerned." He cupped her cheek with his hand. "But you don't have the stress of a shaky marriage to deal with this time, and you're already further along than you've ever been before. Right?"

"Right."

He hugged her close. "Then I'd say a celebration is in order, wouldn't you?"

For the first time since he'd entered the apartment, she smiled, making him feel like the sun had come out on a rainy day. "I guess so."

"Go wash your face and change clothes," he said. "I'm taking you out."

"Where are we going?"

"You'll see," he said, grinning.

"What are we doing *here?*" Elena asked, when he parked the Jag in front of Baby World.

"We're going to make this baby thing more real for you," he said, opening the driver's door. He gave her the grin that always made her stomach flutter. "Besides, Peanut is going to need a bed."

"But I'm—" She waited for him to come around the front of the car to open her door. "I'm not ready for baby furniture. I have to clear out the spare bedroom, paint—"

"Forget painting." He took her by the elbow and led her to the entrance of the brightly lit store. "It's not good for the baby. We'll pick out wallpaper while we're here.''

Elena dug in her heels, forcing him to stop just inside the double doors of the store. ''How do you know what's good for a baby and what isn't, Connelly?''

''I read all about it in the magazine you gave me the other day in the doctor's office,'' he said, his grin smug. He turned to look at the huge display room. ''Now, what colors do you want for the nursery?''

She laughed and shook her head. ''You read one magazine article and you think you're an expert. You're impossible.''

''Impossibly amazing,'' he said, sounding quite confident and more than a little pleased with himself. ''Now, let's see what this place has to offer in the way of baby stuff.''

''I'm not buying anything tonight,'' she warned him.

''That's okay.'' He took her by the hand and led her toward the furniture department on the far side of the store. ''We'll just look and see what they have.''

Elena shook her head as she followed Brett through several full nursery displays. How could she be angry with the man? He'd come running when he thought there was something seriously wrong, had seemingly understood her ridiculous reasons for feeling lower than dirt, then kept her laughing with outrageous questions and comments about what purpose the different items of baby furniture served.

''Did you see anything you liked?'' he asked as they stood looking at the last color-coordinated set.

Pointing several displays over, she nodded. ''The yellow-and-white ensemble was my favorite. It's bright and cheerful and the light oak furniture is beautiful.''

"Then yellow-and-white are your nursery colors," he said, leading her out of the furniture department and into an area filled with shelves of stuffed animals. He let go of her hand to examine some of the toys. "What do you think Peanut will like more, bears or bunnies?"

"I don't know," she said, laughing as he rubbed several of the toys against his lean cheek. "What are you doing?"

"Checking for softness." He sneezed. "That one sheds." He placed the furry rabbit back on the shelf, then picked up a large white bear with a yellow gingham ribbon around its neck. Apparently satisfied by the feel of its fur against his skin, he grinned. "I like this one."

"Babe is going to be jealous," she warned.

He held the bear in the crook of one arm, took Elena by the hand and headed for the checkout. "This isn't for me. It's for you until Peanut arrives." He stopped suddenly to put his finger under her chin and tilt her face until their gazes met. "Every time you look at this bear, I want you to remember that you have Peanut inside of you and that your dream of being a mother will come true. That he—"

"She," Elena corrected him.

He grinned. "Or *she* will be here very soon."

Touched by his thoughtfulness, Elena swallowed around the lump in her throat. "Thank you, Brett." A tear slowly trickled down her cheek.

"Don't cry, honey," he said, wiping it away with the pad of his thumb. "It's just a teddy bear."

"It's not the bear, silly. It's the gesture. This is one

of the sweetest, most thoughtful things anyone's ever done for me.'' Reaching up, she placed a kiss on his cheek. "Thank you."

On Valentine's Day afternoon, Brett sat at his desk, staring out the window at Lake Michigan. He wanted to do something for Elena, but couldn't figure out what that something should be.

All she had were difficult memories to represent the day, and this one didn't seem to be shaping up any better. Not only did it mark the anniversary of the breakup of her marriage, her ex-husband's child was scheduled to be born today.

How could he take the focus off the past and make the day something she'd remember fondly? How could he go about doing that without getting more emotionally involved than he already was?

Deciding that taking her out for dinner was about the best he could do, Brett paged Fiona and told her to make reservations at one of Chicago's most exclusive restaurants.

But fifteen minutes later he pressed the off button on his intercom with a curse. Every place Fiona had called was booked solid, and some even had a waiting list.

Frustrated, he glanced around the room, his gaze coming to rest on the collage of family pictures hanging on the far wall. As he stared at the photo of himself and Drew taken the summer they built their cabin on the family property up at Lake Geneva, an idea began to form.

Satisfied that he'd found the perfect solution, Brett picked up the phone and made the arrangements, then walked down the hall to the conference room. He knew exactly how to get Elena to accompany him without tipping her off that he had something up his sleeve.

When he entered the room, he found her alone. "I need to talk to you."

"Do you even know how to knock, Connelly?" she asked, looking up from her notes. The smile she wore took the sting out of her words. "You're lucky my last interview just left, or I'd be forced to arrest you for obstructing an investigation."

He barely resisted the urge to hold out his wrists for her to cuff him. Instead, he adopted what he hoped was a worried expression. "I just got a call that my cabin up on Lake Geneva may have been broken into. I'm headed up there to check it out. Would you like to go along in case it has something to do with your investigation?"

Her smile vanished. "Of course." She stood and quickly gathered her notes. "How did you find out about the break-in?"

He hated lying to her. "The caretaker didn't say it was a break-in exactly, just that it looked like someone had been inside."

"Have you notified the authorities up there?"

"No."

She gave him a suspicious look. "Why not?"

He blinked. What reason could he give her? Naturally, if there had been the possibility of a real break-in that was the first thing he'd have done.

Think, Connelly.

"I, uh, thought you might want to check it out first," he said, hoping his excuse made sense. "You know, on the outside chance there's evidence that someone unfamiliar with the case would overlook."

"Or inadvertently destroy while checking things out," she said, agreeing with him. "That's happened more times than I care to count."

Brett glanced at his watch. "If we leave now, we should get up there with plenty of daylight left to look around." He took her coat from the brass coat tree by the door and holding it for her, added, "It might not be a bad idea if we change clothes before we head up that way."

She turned to face him. "Why?"

Giving himself a mental pat on the back for having a logical answer this time, he said, "It's cold and there's a lot of snow on those rural roads. If we get stuck, I'd rather we have on heavier clothing than what we wear to the office."

"Good point." She glanced down at her black suit coat and matching skirt. "Jeans and a sweatshirt would definitely be more practical."

Guiding her out of the conference room, Brett congratulated himself on his plan and the skillful way he'd executed it. Everything was going off without a hitch.

Elena hoped Brett's visibility was better from the driver's side of the car than from where she sat in the passenger seat. The snow flurries that had started falling as they left Chicago had turned into a full-fledged blizzard by the time they'd reached the Wisconsin state line.

"Can you see where you're going?" she asked.

"Barely," he said, shifting the car into a lower gear and steering it off the main road onto a narrow lane. "The weather report said this storm front wouldn't move through for days."

When Babe whined from her spot between Elena's feet, Elena reached down to give the little dog a reassuring pat on the head. "Somebody at the weather service missed this forecast."

"Obviously," Brett muttered, navigating the tree-lined road.

The snow slacked off a bit, and in the approaching twilight of late afternoon, Elena could see the shape of a large house through the branches of the leafless trees. "Is that the cabin?" she asked incredulously.

"That's it." When the low-slung car came to an abrupt stop, he muttered an oath. "We're stuck in a snowdrift. We'll have to walk the rest of the way."

"Some cabin," she said, staring at the impressive structure. "I've seen smaller apartment buildings."

"I never really thought about it," he said, shrugging. "You don't like it?"

She shook her head. "I didn't say that. It's just not as small or as rustic as I expected it to be."

He grinned as he reached for the door handle. "Well, it's made out of logs."

She stared at the two-and-a-half-story house. "So this is where your family vacations?"

"Nope." Getting out of the car, he waded through the drift to open the passenger door. "My mom and dad's cottage is on the other side of the property. This belongs to me and Drew. After his wife died, we spent the following summer up here putting it together."

"You two built it?"

Nodding, he admitted, "We had a crew helping us position the logs and put up the trusses, but we worked right along with them. And we did the majority of the interior work ourselves."

"I'm impressed," she said, truly meaning it.

He looked puzzled. "Why? Log homes come as precut kits and all we had to do was put it together."

"Yes, but that took a lot of work for something this big," she said, handing him Babe. "I don't guess I thought of you as the type to enjoy physical labor."

As he took the dog from her, he leaned forward to whisper close to her ear. "Don't tell anyone, but I enjoy a lot of physical activities. And I'm *very* good at most of them."

Tingles of excitement raced through her at the feel of his warm breath on her skin and the insinuation of what else he was good at doing. "I'll take your word on that," she said, feeling her cheeks color.

Get your mind back to business, Delgado. Thinking about Brett in any way other than being a friend could prove disastrous.

She reached into her handbag to remove her service revolver, but when she stepped out of the car into the snow, Brett blocked her path. He set Babe down, then stood with his fists planted on his lean hips.

"What do you think you're doing?" he asked.

"I'm preparing to investigate a potential crime scene." She pushed at his chest to get him to move. It didn't do a bit of good. The man was built rock solid and wasn't about to budge. "What's wrong with you, Brett? We came up here to check out—"

"Put the gun away," he demanded.

She shook her head. "If there's been a break-in—"

"There hasn't been." Before she realized what he was doing, Brett reached out and took the gun from her, then shoved it into his jacket pocket. "But if there had been, there's no way I'd let you go in there

ahead of me.'' He turned around and bent down.
''Climb on my back.''

''I can walk.''

''No, you can't.'' He reached behind him to place
his hands behind her thighs and pulled her up and
onto his back.

Surprised by his sudden move, she had to link her
arms around his neck in order to steady herself. ''Put
me down.''

''No.''

''What's going on here, Connelly?''

''I'm giving you a piggyback ride.''

She tried not to enjoy the feel of her breasts pressed
to his strong back. ''If someone is in there—''

He started walking toward the cabin. ''Trust me.
There isn't.''

''You don't know for sure, unless—'' She gasped.
''This is a setup, isn't it?''

Brett stopped trudging through the snow and turned
his head to glance over his shoulder at her. ''It sure
is.''

He walked the few short yards to the wraparound
deck and bent down to lower her to her feet. Unlock-
ing the door, he turned to cup her cheek with his
palm. The look in his blue eyes took her breath. ''I
wanted you to have something good to remember
about Valentine's Day.''

Struck speechless, Elena followed when he took
her by the hand and led her through the house and
into the huge great room. Distracted by Babe racing
by them to dive under the pillows on the leather sofa
in front of the big stone fireplace, she needed a moment to notice the table set for two in front of the
wall of windows overlooking the lake.

Tears filled her eyes. A single white taper in a silver holder sat in the center of the table, the ring of red roses surrounding its base adding a splash of color to the white linen tablecloth.

"Oh, Brett," she said, turning to look at him. He held his arms out, and she didn't think twice about walking into his embrace. "No one has ever done anything this nice for me."

"Please tell me these are happy tears," he said, holding her close.

"They are." She leaned back to look up at him. "Why did you do it?"

His smile warmed her insides and caused her toes to curl. "Because you deserve it." He wiped the tears from her cheeks. "And because I wanted to do something that you could look back on with fond memories."

"Thank you, Brett," she said, wondering how she could ever have thought him to be anything like Michael.

She reached up on tiptoe to give him a brief kiss, but the moment their lips met, he pulled her to him and took control. His firm lips moved over hers with such exquisite thoroughness that heat streaked to every cell in her body. His tongue traced her mouth, asking her permission, letting her know that he wanted to take the caress further. Without hesitation she opened for him. She wanted the feel of his tongue mating with hers, wanted to savor the taste that was uniquely Brett.

As soon as he slipped inside to tease and stroke, her knees felt as if they'd turned to jelly, and she had to wrap her arms around his neck to keep from melting into a puddle at his feet. She moaned when he pressed himself to her, allowing her to feel the hard ridge of his arousal, his growing need for her.

Holding her close, he slowly slid one hand beneath the tail of her sweater, then brought it up to gently cup her breast. The heat of his strong palm holding her, the pad of his thumb teasing her sensitive nipple through the lace of her bra, created an aching need deep inside, and Elena gasped at the strength of the feeling.

"It's all right, honey," he said, trailing kisses from her mouth to the column of her throat. "Nothing is going to happen that you don't want to happen."

Momentarily incapable of speech, she could only nod.

He removed his hand and smoothed her sweater back into place, then gazed down at her with slumberous navy eyes. "I want you to sit down and relax while I go check on our dinner."

"Is there anything I can do to help?" she asked finally, making her vocal chords work.

He shook his head. "No. I'm going to take care of everything. This evening is just for you. All you have to do is enjoy it."

When he kissed the tip of her nose and turned to light the logs in the fireplace, Elena bit her lower lip as reality began to invade her thoughts. They were in a remote area of the Connelly property on Lake Geneva. It was still snowing, and the car was stuck in a drift. Their chances of returning to the city before sometime tomorrow were down to zero and sinking. And they wanted each other.

A shiver of intense longing coursed through her at the thought. Not even in the four years of her marriage had the desire to be intimate with a man been this intense.

She wrapped her arms around herself and turned to stare at the table for two, the candle's dancing flame reflected in the windows overlooking the lake. They were stranded, the setting couldn't be more romantic and there was an attraction between them that bordered on explosive.

If that wasn't a recipe for destroying her peace of mind and breaking her heart, she didn't know what was.

Eight

Brett watched Elena over the flicker of candlelight and wondered how he was ever going to keep his hands to himself. She was absolutely gorgeous and the most desirable woman he'd ever known. And the irony of it all was that she didn't even realize it.

She had no way of knowing that the soft glow of the candle's flame made him want to see her lying gloriously nude in his bed, her satiny skin glistening with perspiration from their lovemaking. Nor did she realize how watching her sweet, perfect mouth sip sparkling white grape juice from a champagne glass made him want her lips kissing him, tasting him as he wanted to taste her.

When she picked up a chocolate-covered strawberry, bit into it, then licked the juice from her fingers with the tip of her tongue, he swallowed hard and barely suppressed a groan. What had he been thinking when he'd called Sam, the Connelly's Lake Geneva caretaker, and asked if the man's wife, Rosie, could prepare a Valentine's dinner for two? What made him think that he could remain detached from the situation? And how the hell was he going to survive when the second phase of his plan was executed?

Brett had no doubt that Elena would love it. But he'd already suffered heart palpitations from the kiss they'd shared earlier. If she kissed him like that again, he wasn't sure he'd be able to stop himself from throwing her over his shoulder, carrying her upstairs and ravishing her lovely body for the rest of the night.

Of course, her reaction—the surprise and happiness he'd seen in her beautiful brown eyes—when they'd first walked into the cabin had been worth it. He'd known for sure that he'd accomplished his mission. He'd given her a Valentine's Day memory that she could look back on without sadness or regret. That alone was well worth whatever hell he had to go through.

Glancing out the windows at the lake, he noticed that the flurries had stopped and the clouds had cleared, allowing the moon and stars to cast a soft-blue glow over the newly fallen snow. Sam should be arriving any minute to pick them up.

As if on cue the doorbell rang.

"You weren't expecting anyone, were you?" Elena asked, frowning.

Brett couldn't help but smile at her cautious expression. "Always the suspicious detective, aren't you?" He rose, then held out his hand. "Come with me."

"What have you got up your sleeve this time, Connelly?" she asked. But she trustingly placed her hand in his, and the touch of her soft palm sent his blood pressure soaring. He might just have to strip down and roll around in the snow in order to cool his libido.

Taking their coats from the closet beside the door, he held hers out for her. "Close your eyes."

"What are you—"

"Hush," he said, placing his finger to her lips. "Trust me. You'll like this last surprise."

When she looked up at him, Brett swallowed hard. She did trust him. He could tell. But if she only knew what deliciously wicked scenario had been running through his mind just moments ago as he gazed at her over the flicker of the candle, she would probably use her gun on him.

He quickly placed his hand over her eyes before she had a chance to read the desire he was sure blazed in his. Putting his arm around her shoulder, he led her outside and down the steps.

As they passed Sam and Rosie, the middle-aged man nodded and gave Brett a grin. "Nice night, isn't it?"

"Who's that?" Elena asked, turning her head in the man's direction.

"Elena, I'd like you to meet Sam and Rosie," Brett said, removing his hand from her eyes. "Sam takes care of the houses and grounds for us here at Lake Geneva, and Rosie is the best cook in southern Wisconsin."

"It's nice to meet you, Sam," Elena said, shaking the hand of the man in front of her. Turning to Rosie, she asked, "Are you the one responsible for that delicious dinner?"

"Yes, ma'am," Rosie said, beaming. "Did you find it to your liking?"

Elena smiled and placed her hand over her stomach. "It was heavenly and I'm positively stuffed."

She wondered why Brett had made meeting the couple such a big secret, until Sam took a step back. "Ready to go for your ride?"

Elena's gaze followed the sweeping gesture of his hand to the horse-drawn sleigh behind him. "Oh, my Lord!" she gasped, covering her mouth with both hands.

"Do you like the rest of my surprise?" Brett whispered close to her ear.

Throwing her arms around his neck, she kissed his cheek. "I love it. It's so…so wonderful."

"Don't cry," he said quickly. "In this temperature your tears will turn to little ice cubes." He placed a kiss on her forehead and helped her climb into the antique black sleigh. Seating himself beside her, he pulled several heavy blankets over their laps, then took up the reins. "We won't be too long," he said to Sam.

The man nodded as he slapped the chestnut-colored horse on the rump. "Take your time and have a nice ride. Rosie and I will take care of cleaning up while you're gone."

Elena watched the couple start up the steps to the deck. "They seem so nice."

Brett nodded. "They are. They've worked for us since before Drew and I were born."

As he guided the horse onto the lane, Elena's attention was captured by the sights and sounds of the wintry night. Moonlight shining through the naked tree branches cast an ethereal glow over the landscape. The swish of the sleigh runners sliding over the snow and the horse's muffled hoofbeats were the only sounds interrupting the otherwise silent night.

"It's like something out of a fairy tale," Elena whispered. "It's magical."

"You deserve magic," Brett said, turning his head to smile at her. The expression on his handsome face told her that he meant every word of what he'd said, and she lost a little bit more of her heart to the man who had given her the Valentine's Day memory of a lifetime.

They rode in easy silence for some time before he turned the horse onto a path that led off through the woods. The darker shadows of the thick trees blotted out the moonlight and lent an intimacy to the quiet night that made Elena feel as if the world had been reduced to just the two of them.

"Where does this lead?" she asked, snuggling closer to him.

"Down to a little cove," he answered, his deep baritone sending a shiver up her spine that had nothing to do with the chilly air. As the sleigh emerged from the tree-lined trail, Brett drew the horse to a stop and pointed toward the lake ahead. "I thought you might like to see this."

Stars twinkled above, and the moon shone brightly over the frozen surface of Lake Geneva. The powdery white snow covering the shoreline glistened in the moonlight, making it look as if diamond dust had been cast over everything.

Elena's breath caught at the sight. "Brett, it's beautiful!"

"I thought you'd like it," he said, putting his arm around her to draw her closer.

They stared at the picture-perfect landscape for several long minutes before she kissed his lean cheek. "I love it. I don't think I've ever seen anything more breathtaking. Thank you for sharing it with me."

"I've seen something more breathtaking," he said, lowering his head to hers. "You."

Holding the reins in one gloved hand, he cupped her face with the other, then brought his mouth down on hers. Excitement instantly tingled every nerve in her body as he gently traced the outline of her lips, then slipped his tongue inside to stroke her with a featherlight touch. The kiss was so sweet, yet so provocative that Elena felt deep need begin to coil in the pit of her stomach.

Brett secured the leather reins to the front of the sleigh, then took her into his arms. Holding her close, he kissed his way from her cheek down to the sensitive hollow behind her ear.

"You're so soft, so sweet," he murmured against her skin.

Unbuttoning her coat, he slipped his hand inside. But when he cupped her breast, they both groaned in frustration at the barriers of her heavy sweater and his leather glove.

"We need to be getting back," he finally said, leaning back to draw her coat together. "I don't want you to get chilled."

She nodded as she tried to get her breathing to return to normal. "It would probably be best. But I don't think you have to worry about my getting cold. At the moment, I'm feeling quite warm."

He chuckled as he dropped a kiss on the tip of her nose. "Me, too." Taking up the reins again, he steered the horse onto the path leading back to the lane. Brett was quiet for several long moments before he said, "You do realize we'll have to spend the night here."

"I had that much figured out," she admitted. "It's probably going to take quite a bit of digging to get your car out of that drift."

He shrugged. "Sam can bring the tractor over and pull it out in the morning. I'd ask him to do it tonight, but it's getting late. Besides, by tomorrow morning the road crews should have everything plowed." She heard him inhale deeply, then as if coming to a decision, he added, "I want you to know that I didn't bring you up here with seduction in mind."

"I never thought you did," she said, meaning it. Brett had never tried to hide his attraction to her, but he'd never taken it any further than a few heated kisses.

He nodded. "I meant what I said earlier, Elena. I won't do anything you don't want me to. You're safe with me." He paused for a moment, then continued. "But I think it's only fair to warn you that when we get back to the cabin, I'm going to have a hell of a time keeping my hands off you." He turned his head to look at her, and the desire she saw in his dark blue eyes took her breath away. "I want you, Elena."

She thought about what he said for the rest of the ride back to his house. A mental image of Brett's hands on her body, caressing, teasing, coaxing, sent a delicious heat racing straight to the pit of her stomach.

Did she want to continue keeping Brett at arm's length? Or did she want him to take her into his arms and show her how deeply his passion ran. Did she want to allow herself to revel in making love with the man she'd fallen in love with?

Time seemed to stand still at the knowledge that she'd fallen in love with Brett Connelly. How could she have let that happen? Hadn't she sworn never to give another man that kind of power over her—the ability to devastate her emotionally?

She glanced over at him as he skillfully steered the horse along the snow-packed lane. She'd tried her best to keep her distance from him. But he'd made that an impossible task.

From the moment they met, he'd gone out of his way to lend her the support and encouragement that she'd never known. He'd stayed with her at the hospital when she'd feared losing her baby, then later opened his home to her when he learned she had nowhere else to go. He'd gone out of his way to make sure she took care of herself and didn't overdo things. He expressed a genuine concern for her safety and had taken it upon himself to squire her around the city as if he had nothing better to do.

He'd even been with her for the first glimpse of the life growing inside of her. And although she was sure he hadn't fully understood why it bothered her, Brett had helped her overcome the self-doubt that she'd suffered at the news of her ex-husband and his new wife having a child.

How could a woman not fall head over heels for a man who had appointed himself her own personal white knight? A man who went out of his way to replace bad Valentine's memories with good ones?

When Brett pulled the horse to a stop by the steps of the deck, Elena looked around. She'd been so lost in thought, they'd arrived back at his cabin without her even realizing it.

"Did Brett show you the cove?" Rosie asked as she and Sam stepped out of the house onto the deck.

"Yes, he did," Elena answered. She placed her hands on Brett's shoulders as he helped her down from the sleigh. "It was quite beautiful."

"I always love taking a ride down there right after it snows," the woman said, looking expectantly at Sam.

Chuckling, Sam shook Brett's hand. "Looks like we'll be taking the long way back to the lodge."

Brett grinned mischievously. "You two kids have fun."

Sam laughed as he helped Rosie into the sleigh. "We will."

"I put the leftovers in the fridge, and Sam walked your dog, Brett," Rosie said, holding the blankets so Sam could climb in beside her.

"Thanks for helping me this evening on such short notice," Brett said.

Settling himself on the seat beside his wife, Sam nodded. "I'll be over here in the morning to pull your car out with the tractor."

Elena felt warmed all over when Brett looked at her for several long moments. The question in his eyes was undeniable and with a slight nod of her head, she gave him her answer.

Brett turned back to Sam. "Make it around noon."

"Will do," the man said, slapping the horse's rump with the reins. "Good night."

"'Night," Rosie called, waving as she and Sam started down the lane.

"Let's go inside the house and get warm," Brett said, taking Elena by the hand.

As soon as they walked into the cabin, he helped

her out of her coat, took off his own, then motioned her toward the great room. "Why don't you warm yourself by the fire, while I hang these up and make some hot cocoa?"

"Do you want me to help?" she asked.

"No." Touching her cheek with his index finger, he drew it down the line of her jaw, his gentle touch causing her breath to come out in shallow little puffs. "This evening is all for you, honey. I'm going to take care of everything."

Elena watched him hang their coats in the closet, then turn and walk toward the kitchen. He was giving her time to think about her decision, giving her time to change her mind. But that wasn't going to happen.

"Brett?"

"Yes?"

"I don't want cocoa."

The light in his eyes as he turned to face her caused heat to pool between her legs. "What do you want, Elena?" he asked, his voice deeper than it had been only seconds before.

"I want you," she said simply.

He walked up to her and drew her into his arms. "Once we go upstairs, there won't be any turning back," he warned. "I want you too much." His gaze caressed her face. "When we close the bedroom door I'm going to take off our clothes and make love to you until we're both exhausted."

"I'm going to hold you to that," she said, hardly recognizing her own voice. What else could she say? She wanted him in every way a woman could want a man.

Without another word, Brett stepped back, took her by the hand and led her up the planked staircase and into a huge bedroom. Closing the door behind them, he guided her over to stand in front of a pair of French doors on the far side of the room. He brushed her lips with his, then he opened the drapes to allow moonlight to flood the room with the same ethereal glow that it had cast on the snow at the cove.

"I want to see you bathed in moonbeams," he said, coming back to stand in front of her. "And I want you to see me."

Capturing her gaze with his, he reached for the end of her burgundy cable-knit sweater. "Hold your arms up for me, honey," he said as he slowly, carefully drew the garment up and over her head. He tossed it on a chair to one side of the doors, then unbuttoned her shirt.

When she placed her hands on the band of his sweatshirt, he shook his head. "Remember, you don't have to do anything but let me love you," he said, quickly pulling the shirt off to toss it on the chair with hers.

Elena's eyes widened at the sight of his sculptured physique. Reaching out, she reverently touched his smooth skin, the hard muscle beneath her fingers flexing and bunching as she lightly traced the ridges and plains of his chest and flat stomach. "You're beautiful."

"Not me," he said, parting her shirt to push it from her shoulders. His sharp intake of breath made her glad that she hadn't bothered with a bra. "You're the one who's beautiful."

He brought his hands up to cup her breasts, to tease her with his thumbs. Her nipples immediately hardened into pebbles of pure sensation and Brett leaned

down to kiss each one with such tenderness it brought
tears to her eyes.

He stepped back to shed the rest of his clothing,
and she knew he was revealing himself to her first, in
order to make her feel less vulnerable. Her heart
swelled with love at his concession.

Turning to face her, he smiled, and the butterflies
in her stomach went wild. Heat, combined with a delicious fluttering, pooled in the pit of her stomach,
and her knees felt as if they might not support her.
He was absolutely gorgeous.

Wide shoulders tapered down to lean flanks and
narrow hips. Her gaze dropped lower. The strength of
his thick arousal rising proudly from the patch of
black curls at his groin caused her heart to stall. He
wasn't a small man.

He must have read the sudden hesitance in her
eyes. "You aren't frightened of me, are you, Elena?"

She shook her head. "It's not that I'm afraid exactly. It's just been a long time since—"

"It's going to be all right, honey." He stepped forward to thread his fingers in her shoulder-length hair.
Tilting her head up, he smiled when their gazes met.
"We'll take this slow and easy. I'm going to make
sure everything is perfect for you. Trust me?"

When she nodded, he stepped back and knelt before her to pull off her boots and socks. Straightening,
he brought his index finger up to touch the valley
between her breasts, then trail it down her body to
the snap on her jeans. He unfastened and unzipped
the denim, then, catching her gaze with his, he slowly,
carefully pushed them and her cotton panties from her
hips.

Elena shivered at the heated look he gave her when

she stepped out of them. "You're perfect," he said, taking her into his arms.

He gently drew her forward until their bodies met, and she could feel her breasts pressed against his hard chest. The touch of skin to skin sent tiny sparks of pleasure skipping along every nerve in her body. She circled his neck with her arms and marveled at the man holding her.

The warm strength of his much larger body, the smell of his spicy cologne and the sound of his harsh breathing all combined to tighten the coil of desire deep inside of her. His hands caressed her back as he ran them the length of her spine to cup her bottom and pull her forward. She couldn't stop a tiny moan from escaping when his heated arousal came into contact with her soft belly.

Brett's answering groan let her know he was experiencing the same intense pleasure, feeling the same exquisite need. "You're so warm, so soft..." His lips brushed hers. "So sweet."

Closing his eyes, Brett took several deep breaths. He wanted Elena more than he'd ever wanted any woman, and it was going to take every ounce of control he'd ever possessed in order to take things slowly.

Incapable of speech, he brought his mouth down on hers to show her what he was feeling, to let her know how beautiful he thought she was and how much her trust meant to him. Her soft lips molded to his almost desperately, firing his blood and sending it surging through his veins with the speed of a raging river.

Her soft sigh allowed him entry to her sweetness, and he thought the top of his head might just come off when her small tongue boldly met his. She was answering him, letting him know that she felt the passion as keenly as he did.

Breaking the kiss, he led her to the bed and turned down the covers. She stared at him wordlessly for one long moment, then slid between the pristine sheets. His heart stalled, then slammed against his ribs with brutal force when she raised her arms in an age-old welcome.

It was then that his lack of planning hit him between the eyes. He hadn't anticipated making love with Elena and therefore hadn't planned for protection. But as he looked down at the woman inviting him into her arms, her very body, he realized there was no possibility of his making her pregnant. And it wouldn't matter to him if she wasn't already pregnant.

For the first time in his life, the thought of fathering a child somehow appealed to something deep inside him. It was something he didn't entirely understand and, at the moment, didn't want to.

Without another second's hesitation, he slid into bed beside her and gathered her into his arms. Desire thrummed through his veins, and he had to fight the urge to cover her with his body, to sink himself deep within her sweet depths. This was Elena's night, and if it killed him, he wasn't going to rush things, no matter what his body demanded.

When Brett pulled her to him, he pulsed with desire. He'd never felt anything so intense, so urgent as the need to claim her.

He trailed kisses down to the base of her throat, then past her collarbone to the slope of her breast. She threaded her fingers in his thick hair and held him to her when he took the hardened peak into his mouth. Sparkles of light much like the stars in the inky night sky outside flashed behind his closed lids when she arched her back to give him easier access to her sensitive flesh.

"Please," she whimpered.

Her body heated with a need that stole her breath. If Brett didn't make love to her soon and end the sweet torture, Elena knew for sure she'd go mad.

"Not yet, honey," he said, lifting his head to look at her. "I want you to remember this night for the rest of your life."

She could have told him that he'd already given her a night she'd never forget, but words failed her. He was trailing his hand down her side to her hip and beyond. He cupped her mound of curls, parting her to stroke the tight nub of pleasure, then dip his finger inside.

Tears filled her eyes from the pleasure of his intimate touch. "I need you, Brett," she said, her voice little more than a whisper. "Now."

His breathing was as ragged as hers as he nudged her knees apart and levered himself over her. He kissed her tenderly and moved his lower body into position. At the first touch of his blunt tip, the coil inside her tightened unbearably.

"Look at me, Elena," he said, his voice sounding like a rusty hinge.

He held her gaze with his and slowly, carefully pushed himself forward. Her body seemed to melt around him as he sank deeper and deeper into her. Never had she felt so filled, so exquisitely stretched. She raised her hips for more of him and when he was buried completely, she sighed at the pleasure of being one with him.

"So tight," he said between clenched teeth.

He eased his hips back then forward, thrusting into her again and again, increasing the rhythm with each stroke. She wrapped her legs around his lean waist in an effort to get closer, and the pressure of his body pressed so intimately with hers had her poised at the edge of fulfillment.

Brett must have recognized her readiness because he thrust deeply into her one last time, causing her body to be swept up in wave upon wave of satisfaction.

A groan rumbled up from deep in his chest and his big body shuddered as he poured himself into her, then collapsed from the force of his own climax.

Reality slowly descended on Brett, and it was several minutes before he found the strength to move to Elena's side. Gathering her protectively against him, he knew for certain he'd just experienced the most powerful lovemaking of his life. Never had his pleasure been more intense, more debilitating than with Elena. And although it scared the hell out of him, it also made him feel complete in a way he'd never felt before.

"Are you all right?" he asked, gently touching the soft roundness of her stomach.

"Yes," she said, her breath feathering his chest as she spoke. "That was incredible."

Chuckling, he nodded. "I couldn't agree more."

She yawned, and he realized that she had to be exhausted. The magazine he'd read in the doctor's office had said that expectant mothers required more sleep in the first and last months of a pregnancy.

Brett kissed the top of her head, then pulled the sheet and comforter over them. "Rest now, honey."

He'd no sooner said the words than he realized Elena had already drifted off into a peaceful sleep.

Staring at the ceiling, Brett held her close and thought about the feelings that coursed through him. He'd never before felt this way after making love to a woman. The degree of possessiveness coursing through him was so strong it was almost palpable.

Absently stroking the soft skin of her lower belly, he thought about the emotional attachment that he'd let form for Elena and Peanut. He tried to remind himself that relationships were dangerous, that unless he wanted to risk suffering the same hell his twin brother had suffered, he'd do well to distance himself now. But the thought of not being with Elena, of taking her back to Chicago and asking his father to assign one of his other siblings to the task of helping her with the interviews, was unthinkable.

It was a completely new and alien concept to him, and one he wasn't at all comfortable with. But he wanted to be with her, wanted to be a part of her and Peanut's lives.

He just wished he knew how to go about doing that without risking his heart in a relationship that he knew for certain would destroy him if Elena ever walked away.

Nine

The sun was turning the early-morning sky to pearl gray when Elena opened her eyes to look over at the man sleeping beside her. Brett had awakened her during the night to make love to her again, and her feelings for him increased tenfold each time they came together. She'd never known a man who put her pleasure before his, who was more concerned with pleasing her than satisfying himself.

Of course, there had only been Michael before Brett, and even though she'd first thought they were exactly alike, she'd quickly learned there was no comparison between the two men. Michael was a shallow, self-centered playboy with nothing on his mind but his own selfish pleasure, while Brett had depth and character and went out of his way to see to her welfare and happiness.

From the moment they met, Brett had been there

for her in a way she wasn't used to. He'd taken care of her when she'd pushed herself too hard with work, been there with her to share the happiness at the doctor's office and comforted her when she'd let her fears get the best of her. Brett had seen her at her most vulnerable, yet it hadn't caused him to run in the opposite direction as it would have with Michael.

No, Brett and Michael were worlds apart, and it was past time to admit that she loved Brett in a way that she'd never loved Michael.

Easing from beneath Brett's arm where it draped her stomach, Elena got out of bed, gathered her clothes and went into the master bathroom for a quick shower. It was going to take time to get used to the idea of loving again, of putting her faith and trust in another man.

She'd just stepped beneath the refreshing spray when the shower door opened and Brett stepped inside. "What are you doing here?" she demanded, suddenly feeling self-conscious. She wasn't sure, but she had a good idea that moonlight streaming through a bedroom window was much more flattering than the bright lights of a bathroom.

"I missed you," he said.

He must have noticed her apprehension, because he took her into his arms and kissed her until the world spun dizzily around her. When he raised his head, he smiled that charming smile that never failed to set the butterflies fluttering wildly in her stomach.

"You're beautiful."

"So are you," she said breathlessly, deciding there was no lighting, natural or artificial, that could make Brett look anything less than perfect.

Without a word he released her to pick up the soap

from the built-in holder in the shower wall and, rubbing it into a rich lather, he ran it over her back then around to her chest. He placed the soap back in the soap dish, then cupped her breasts with his soapy hands. His gaze caught hers, and the desire in his eyes, his heart-stopping grin as he tenderly circled her nipples with his slick thumbs caused her pulse to race.

As Brett leisurely smoothed his hands over her body, Elena's head fell back and she let the exquisite sensations overtake her. She'd never realized how erotic the simple act of taking a shower could be. But then she'd never had a man bathe her before.

He massaged and soothed, caressed and teased everywhere he touched, and by the time he reached the apex of her thighs, she thought she'd go mad from the need he had created. Pure, electrified desire raced over every nerve in her body as his hands skimmed from her inner thighs to the sensitive folds of her feminine flesh. He placed one arm around her back to steady her, then parted her with his other hand to stroke her intimately.

His mouth came down on hers almost desperately, and she returned his kiss with the same degree of urgency. When his tongue sought and found entry to the inner recesses of her mouth, there was nothing soft or tender about the invasion. He demanded her uninhibited response and she gladly gave it, meeting his advance with a boldness of her own, wordlessly telling him what she wanted.

Unwilling to be denied the pleasure of touching his body as he touched hers, she reached out to encircle his engorged flesh, to measure his length and the strength of his need for her. He shuddered against her as she stroked him, and feminine power, pure and sweet, swept through her.

"We've got to get out of here," he said suddenly. He turned off the shower, then, pulling her with him, he opened the shower door to lower them both to the thick throw rug on the bathroom floor. "I can't wait," he said, his breathing ragged. "I want you now."

"Then take me," she said, positioning herself to cradle him to her.

Brett took hold of her hips and lifting her to him, knelt before her to join their bodies in one smooth stroke. The feel of her body surrounding him, the passion filling her eyes as he made them one sent his blood pressure to an all-time high and made his heart pound against his ribs in a primitive cadence. Her readiness for him, her unbridled response, took him to new heights of arousal and made setting a leisurely pace impossible.

Thrusting into her, he watched passion paint her cheeks a rosy glow, saw her brown eyes darken to deep pools of chocolate as he moved inside her. Never had lovemaking been so urgent, never had it felt so elemental and wild.

Moments later he felt her body tighten around his, saw her squeeze her eyes shut as she reached the peak. Grinding himself against her, he heard her cry of ecstasy a moment before her spasms of release gripped him and pulled him into the same tumultuous storm.

Throwing his head back, he felt as though her body drained him of his essence. With a groan that he barely recognized as his own, he fell forward and, gathering her to him in order to keep from crushing her, rolled to her side.

As they slowly floated back down to the realm of reality, the only sound in the bathroom for several long minutes was that of their labored breathing.

"Are you all right?" he finally managed to ask. "I didn't hurt you, did I?"

"I'm wonderful." She snuggled against him to press her lips to his chest. "That was incredible."

"You're incredible," he said, pulling her up to lie on top of him.

As he gazed into her soft-brown eyes, he realized that he could make love to Elena every day for the rest of his life and never get enough of her, never sate the passion that threatened to consume him every time they came together. And it scared him senseless.

"Let's get off this floor before you get chilled," he said suddenly.

He rose to his feet and pulled her up with him, then took two thick towels from the linen closet. Wrapping one around his waist, he draped the other around her shoulders and gently rubbed the terry cloth along the goose bumps on her upper arms and across her shoulders.

Even touching her through the thick towel wasn't preventing his body from reacting to her nearness. "I'm going to get dressed and take Babe for a walk," he said, needing the chill of the outside air to help cool the heat that was rapidly building within him once again.

Elena smiled, and his knees threatened to buckle. "I think I'll finish the shower that someone so delightfully interrupted," she said, opening the glass door to turn on the faucet.

If she kept looking at him like that, he'd wind up joining her again and Babe would never forgive him.

"I won't be long," he promised, dropping a kiss on her forehead and hurrying from the bathroom before he changed his mind.

Three hours later Elena absently patted Babe's small head as Brett pulled the Jag out of the lane and onto the main road. She hated leaving the winter wonderland of Lake Geneva. It reminded her of her native southern Illinois with its many lakes and lush trees.

Thinking of where she'd grown up reminded her that she hadn't been back to see her foster mother, Marie, in several months. Elena missed the woman who had been the closest thing to a mother that she'd ever known. If not for Marie Waters, Elena knew for certain she wouldn't be the person she was today. Having been abandoned when she was two years old, she'd been shuttled from one foster home to another until, at the age of fourteen, she'd finally been placed with Marie.

Elena smiled fondly at the thought of the woman who had an uncanny knack for accurately judging a person's character in the first few minutes of meeting them. She'd taken one look at Elena and had seen right through the tough exterior and false bravado to the hurting, uncertain teenager within.

Glancing at Brett, Elena wondered what Marie would think of him. She'd certainly been correct in her assessment of Michael Delgado. After meeting him only once, she'd proclaimed him nothing but a shifty-eyed womanizer with few, if any, redeeming qualities.

"What's so funny?" Brett asked, smiling at her.

Unaware that she'd laughed out loud at Marie's

description of her ex-husband, Elena gave him an embarrassed shrug. "Just thinking about Marie."

"That's your foster mother, right?"

She nodded. "She's a real character, and I miss getting to see her as much as I'd like."

"How far away does she live?" he asked, merging onto the interstate highway. He set the cruise control, then switched on the radio to a soft classical station.

"About 325 miles south of Chicago, in Johnston City."

"How often do you get to see her?" he asked, sounding genuinely interested.

"I try to get down there two or three times a year," she said, placing Babe on the floor between her feet. "That's usually the way I spend my vacation time." Leaning back against the seat, she yawned. "I've been thinking about making a trip home after the weather clears up a little more."

He reached over to take her hand in his. "You sound pretty tired."

She smiled. "That's because someone woke me up in the middle of the night and I missed out on a full night's sleep."

"Something came up," he said, his voice sounding so sexy that it made her stomach flutter wildly and her toes curl inside her boots. He brought her hand up to his lips. "We've got another hour's drive. Why don't you try to get a little sleep?"

"I think I will take a nap," she said, removing her hand from his. How could she sleep with him kissing her palm like that, reminding her of how his talented lips had felt on other parts of her body?

Deciding she'd do well not to think about last night, she closed her eyes and settled back against the seat, certain there was no way she'd be able to rest because of the man sitting next to her. But the soft sounds of a harp solo on the radio lulled her with its beauty, and she felt herself start to drift off. Her last thoughts were of Brett and the most memorable Valentine's Day—and night—of her life.

Brett sat in his car in the parking garage at Connelly Tower on Monday morning, his apprehension growing with each passing second. Elena should have arrived twenty minutes ago. He'd tried calling her, both at her apartment and on her cell phone. But the answering machine had picked up at her home number, and he'd gotten voice mail when he dialed her cellular. He hadn't bothered leaving a message on either.

Where could she be? More important, was she all right?

When they returned Friday afternoon from Lake Geneva, there had been a message on Elena's answering machine telling her that her car had been repaired and was ready to be picked up. He'd driven her to the shop. Even though he didn't fully understand why, he didn't like the idea of her driving around the city by herself. The thought of her job taking her into some of the worst neighborhoods in Chicago made his blood run cold.

He'd tried to convince her that car pooling made more sense than both of them driving separately. But she'd laughed and pointed out that he'd have to drive ten minutes in the opposite direction to pick her up. After that, he hadn't been able to come up with another plausible argument why it would be wise to continue letting him drive her. He knew better than to mention the real issue—his concern for her safety. They'd already covered that innumerable times, and she refused to listen to reason.

He checked his watch again. Thirty minutes late. Where could she be? Had she been in an accident? Were she and Peanut all right?

As he sat there trying to decide whether to go looking for her or call the police to report her as missing, her car pulled into an empty visitor's spot on the other side of the garage. Relieved that she hadn't been in an accident, he quickly got out of the car and marched over to her driver's door.

"It's about time," he muttered, his relief quickly turning to anger as he yanked the car door open. "Where the hell were you? You should have been here half an hour ago."

To his further irritation, she leisurely gathered her purse and briefcase before turning to face him. "My, aren't we in a good mood this morning," she said, smiling congenially.

She pushed at his chest to back him up, then got out of the car, locked it and started toward the elevator.

"Well?" he said, shortening his strides to match hers.

"'Well' what?" she asked, punching the call button. While she waited, she stood there humming a tune as if she didn't have a care in the world.

Brett couldn't believe he was letting her bait him, but try as he might, he couldn't seem to stop himself. "I was worried that you might have been in an accident…or worse."

"I wasn't," she said, smiling at him. She was purposely ignoring his bad mood.

When she didn't offer an explanation, he tried to stay calm but found his voice rising with each word. "I tried calling you, but got your answering—"

"So that was you." The elevator doors swished open and she walked inside. "You should have left a message."

Gritting his teeth, he stepped into the car beside her. "You were home and didn't pick up?"

"I was pulling on my panty hose."

"And I don't suppose it occurred to you to stop and pick up the phone," he said, lowering his voice as the elevator opened on the seventeenth floor.

"Actually, it did," she said, stepping out into the corridor. She started walking toward the conference room without elaborating on why she hadn't answered.

"And?" he prompted.

"I didn't want to run the risk of pushing my thumb through my hose or snagging them just to find out it was a telemarketer." She opened the conference room door and strolled over to place her briefcase on the table.

"It never occurred to you that it might be me?" he asked, slamming his briefcase on the polished mahogany surface. He knew he was being unreasonable, but at the moment he didn't care. She'd scared the hell out of him.

"It did occur to me that it might be you." She pulled off her coat to drape it over one of the chairs. "But I thought if it was, you'd leave a message."

He caught her around the waist and pulled her to him. He wasn't sure whether to yell at her for worrying him to the point of distraction or kiss her senseless.

"What the hell," he muttered, bringing his mouth down on hers.

When their lips met, she let loose a startled squeak, and Brett seized the opportunity to plunge his tongue inside. He wanted to punish her for making him worry, wanted to assure himself that she was all right. But the taste of her passion, the smell that was uniquely Elena's sent a jolt of need down his spine to swirl around and explode in his gut. Softening the kiss, he leisurely explored her mouth until they were both gasping for air.

"God, you scared me to death," he said. "Please don't do that again."

"I thought you knew my appointment with Jennifer Anderson wasn't until later this morning," she said, sounding breathless.

Brett thought for a moment, then shook his head. "When you talked to Jennifer, I was in the sunroom with Mom and Dad."

"I'm sorry you were worried, but I was just fine," she said, stepping back to straighten her navy linen suit.

A light tap on the door prevented him from answering, as Fiona stuck her head inside. "Mr. Connelly, Ms. Anderson is here to speak with Ms. Delgado. Would you like me to send her in?"

Before he could answer, Elena stepped around him. "Please give me about five minutes, then send her in, Fiona." Turning back to Brett, she smiled and straightened his tie. Her small hands touched the underside of his chin, causing him to swallow hard. "Just so you don't suffer another anxiety attack, this is my last interview. Unless there's a significant development in the case, I won't be coming back here to Connelly Tower."

Brett's stomach twisted into a painful knot, and he felt as if the floor had dropped from beneath him. He'd purposely avoided thinking about her finishing the interviews, had refused to contemplate what his day would be like without the knowledge that she was right down the hall from him.

Finding the situation totally unacceptable, he picked up his briefcase from the conference table. "We'll talk later." He needed time to think. "Do you have plans for dinner?" he asked suddenly.

"Not really."

"Good." He placed a kiss on the tip of her nose. "Why don't you come by my place around seven? I'll fix some of my famous vegetable lasagna."

"You mean you'll go by Mario's for takeout," she said, laughing.

He grinned. "I'll tell him you said hello."

Elena watched him exchange a pleasant greeting with Jennifer Anderson as he held the door for the young woman to enter the room. Then, winking at Elena behind Jennifer's back, he disappeared down the hall.

Smiling, Elena turned her attention from the man she loved to the young woman walking toward her. "I'm glad you were able to make it," Elena said, extending her hand to the pretty blonde. "I hope you don't mind my asking to meet with you here at Connelly Tower instead of Lake Shore Manor."

"Not at all," Jennifer said, shaking Elena's hand. "It gave me the chance to spend a little more time with my daughter before I had to take her to the day-care center this morning."

"How old is she?" Elena asked, motioning for Jennifer to take a seat at the table.

"Eighteen months," the young woman said proudly. Smiling, she asked, "When is your baby due?"

"I'm due in August. How did you know?" Elena hadn't told anyone connected to the Connellys except Brett.

Before Elena could decide on the method of execution she intended to use on him, Jennifer smiled. "You have that pregnant glow about you."

"Oh," Elena said, feeling her cheeks heat. "That's how you knew?"

Jennifer nodded. "What are you hoping for? A boy or a girl?"

Smiling, Elena placed her hand over her stomach. "I'm hoping for a girl."

"That's what I was hoping for when I found out I was pregnant with Sarah." She glanced down at her hands. "Naturally, my husband wanted a boy."

Elena knew the story of Jennifer's police officer husband and how he'd been killed during a drug bust gone sour. Although Elena had never met the man, she'd attended his funeral to show support for a fallen comrade, as had most of Chicago's police force.

"Have you been doing okay?" she asked, reaching out to touch Jennifer's tightly clenched hands.

The pretty young woman took a deep breath, then met Elena's concerned gaze head on. "It's not easy raising a child alone," she said carefully. "There's no one there to share the worries and fears or to help with the 1001 things that taking care of an infant entails."

Elena didn't know what to say. It sounded as

though the woman was warning her of the difficult time she had ahead of her. "I'm sure it isn't easy."

Deep regret shadowed Jennifer's wide green eyes. "But the worst part is having to be away from Sarah while I work." She hurried on to explain. "Please don't get me wrong. I love working for Mrs. Connelly and she's very good about letting me have time off when Sarah is ill. But I really hate missing most of my baby's firsts."

"You mean her first steps?" Elena asked, feeling the woman's pain.

Jennifer nodded. "That and her first word. The first time she pulled herself up to stand. The first time she crawled."

Elena really hadn't considered how she would feel when she had to leave her baby with someone while she worked. She had decided that she'd eventually take a desk job at SIU because of the more regular hours. But she'd thought it would be a few years down the line.

"I'm sorry if I've upset you," Jennifer apologized. "It's really tough taking care of a baby on your own, but I'm sure you'll do fine."

Nodding, Elena admitted, "I'm really looking forward to being a mother, but I still have a few things to work out."

Deciding that she needed to give it a lot more thought once she got home and had the time to give the matter her undivided attention, Elena opened her notebook and picked up her pencil. "Now, what can you tell me about the day someone tried to assassinate King Daniel?"

Ten

Brett glanced at the clock on the microwave. Time to light the candles. Elena should be there in a few minutes, and he wanted everything to be perfect when she arrived.

Touching the flame from the lighter to the wick, he surveyed his efforts. The candles were lit, the sparkling grape juice sat chilling in the silver ice bucket to one side of his chair, and the red rose in the crystal bud vase emitted just the right amount of fragrance.

Satisfied that he'd done everything he could in preparation for her arrival, he walked over to the windows to stare out at the quiet night. Surely Elena would see the wisdom in his proposition. She had to. He'd spent the entire day reviewing options and working out the details, and it had been the only acceptable solution.

When the doorbell rang, he smiled. Time to put his plan into action.

"Good evening, gorgeous," he said, opening the door to sweep her into his arms.

He brought his mouth down on hers but made sure he kept the kiss brief. He didn't want to be distracted from his mission.

"Good evening to you, too, handsome," she said, sounding breathless. Babe bounced around their feet, vying for attention, and Elena bent down to scratch behind the dog's ears.

"I missed you after you left Connelly Tower this afternoon," he said. When she straightened to look at him, he helped her out of her coat.

"I missed you, too," she said. Her soft voice sent his pulse into overdrive.

Brett quickly put his arm around her shoulders and his hand over her eyes. He not only wanted to surprise her, he needed to block her mesmerizing gaze before he forgot about his mission, picked her up and sprinted for the bedroom to make love to her until they both passed out from exhaustion.

She laughed as he led her toward the dining room. "You certainly have a flare for the dramatic, Connelly. What are you up to now?"

"Trust me, you'll like it," he whispered close to her ear. To his immense satisfaction, she shivered against him, and his confidence in his well-thought-out plan grew.

Stopping by her chair, he removed his hand and directed her attention to the table for two with a sweep of his arm. "Welcome to Café Brett."

"Brett, you didn't have to—"

He placed his index finger to her soft lips. "I know I didn't have to do all this. I wanted to."

"Thank you," she said, kissing the tip of his finger.

Seating her, he walked into the kitchen, took their salad plates from the refrigerator, then returned to the dining room. Once he'd set their places, he opened the grape juice, poured them each a goblet and took his seat on the opposite side of the table.

He stared at her for endless seconds. Why the hell was he so nervous? He was one of the best PR men in the business. He was good at selling ideas and negotiating deals. Besides, his plan was foolproof.

"So tell me about your day," he said, picking up his salad fork. His first bite of the leafy mixed greens might as well have been a mouthful of weeds, for all he could taste of them.

She took a sip of her grape juice before she answered. "Let's see, after you left the conference room this morning I had a very interesting talk with Jennifer Anderson." Elena stared at her plate for a moment. When she looked up, Brett saw a good amount of worry clouding her eyes. "I really feel sorry for Jennifer."

"Why?"

"She's having a tough time right now," Elena answered. She placed her fork across the top of her salad plate. "Life hasn't been very fair to her."

"How do you mean?" he asked, collecting their plates to take them to the kitchen.

She waited to answer him until he'd returned with plates of vegetable lasagna and slices of crusty garlic bread. "She's just too young to be carrying so much responsibility."

"I know she has a child," he said, biting off a

piece of the warm garlic bread. He wisely refrained from pointing out that Jennifer was only three years younger than Elena, and that in a few months she'd be in the same position as Jennifer—a working mother, trying to raise her child alone. "Are things really that hard for her?" he asked.

Elena nodded. "After her husband was killed in the line of duty, she not only had to deal with his death, she was pregnant and faced with the responsibility of raising her child alone. Not to mention having to find a job to support herself and the baby."

"To my knowledge Jennifer is paid pretty well for organizing my mom's social schedule," he said thoughtfully. "But if you think it would help, I'll talk to Mom about giving her a raise."

"It's not a money issue." He watched Elena push lasagna around her plate before putting her fork down and leaning back in her chair.

"Then what is it?" he coaxed when she remained silent.

She looked him square in the eye, and he could see that Elena wasn't just talking about Jennifer anymore. She was expressing her own fears as well. "Jennifer has missed out on so much. She wasn't there for her baby's first words, first steps."

Brett set his goblet on the table and reached for Elena's hand. It tore him apart to see the apprehension marring her lovely features, to see her worried about a problem for which he'd already found a solution.

"Come here," he said, scooting his chair back. He tugged on her hand, and she rose to step around to his side of the small table. Settling her on his lap, he wrapped his arms around her and pulled her to his chest. "Don't worry. You and Peanut are going to be just fine."

She sat up to look at him. "Do you really think so?"

"Trust me on this—I know so," he said, nodding.

She put her arms around his neck. "So you've looked into your crystal ball and know what the future holds for me?"

"Something like that."

He couldn't keep from smiling. His plan was going to work without a hitch. Time to make his proposal.

Elena leaned forward, and his pulse took off. So did all of his thoughts. Her soft lips on his were distracting enough, but when she used her tongue to part his mouth and slip inside, he thought he'd have a coronary.

Elena wasn't the least bit shy about letting him know what she wanted. And Brett loved it.

Her tongue stroked and teased his, and her delightful little bottom wiggled against the part of him that was changing so rapidly, making him glad that he'd chosen tailored slacks instead of jeans. He was harder than he'd ever been, and the confines of denim would have been painful.

Restlessness built inside of him and he tried to shift positions, but the dining room chair proved to be extremely restrictive. He wanted them both to have the freedom to once again explore each other with total abandon.

Breaking the kiss, he cradled her to him and stood up. "Let's take this where we can be more comfortable," he said, heading for his bedroom.

She didn't protest, but instead wrapped her arms around his shoulders and pressed her lips to the pulse pounding at the base of his throat. Raining tiny kisses all the way to his ear, she nipped at the lobe, and he thought his knees might give way right then and there.

When he reached the bedroom, Brett shouldered the door closed behind them, then set Elena on her feet at the side of the bed. "You're driving me crazy," he said, hardly recognizing his own voice.

The smile she gave him sent the blood racing through his veins. "It's only fair." She reached up to touch his face. "You drove me out of my mind at the cabin, now it's my turn to send you over the edge."

When she trailed her fingers down the middle of his chest, stopping just above his belt, his heart thumped against his ribs and his stomach muscles tightened. Tugging his shirt free from his trousers, she started at the bottom and slowly, painstakingly slipped each button through its hole. Her hands brushed his abdomen and chest, and by the time she reached the top, Brett found it hard to draw a breath. But when she pushed his shirt from his shoulders, then leaned forward to kiss his chest, he felt as if he might never breathe again.

He reached for her, but she shooed his hands away. "I'm running this show, Connelly. All you have to do is enjoy yourself."

He'd never harbored a lot of sexual fantasies. But he knew for sure that if he had, one of them was about to come true. He'd never been with a woman who took the part of the aggressor, and he found it excited the hell out of him that Elena wanted to do that.

Finding it hard to stand still, Brett placed his hands on her shoulders and rested his forehead against hers. "You're killing me, honey."

"You don't like what I'm doing?" she asked,

bending to remove his shoes and socks, then hers. Straightening, she unbuckled his belt.

He chuckled and shook his head. "I didn't say that."

"What are you saying, Brett?" She kissed his chest again, and a jolt of need shot straight to his groin.

"It…doesn't matter," he finally managed. How was he supposed to think when she was playing with the tab of his zipper?

When she finally unzipped his slacks, then pushed them down his thighs, he took a deep breath to steady himself and stepped out of them. But the air became lodged in his lungs as her soft palms skimmed his legs from ankle to hip and she brought her hands back to the bulge straining the white cotton of his briefs.

His head fell back and he gritted his teeth so hard his jaw ached when she reached out and ran her fingers along the hard ridge of his erection. In all of his twenty-seven years, he never would have believed that a man could be debilitated with one touch of a woman's hand. But then, this wasn't just any woman. This was Elena.

"This…isn't fair," he said through gritted teeth. "I'd like…to return the favor."

She stepped back, shook her head and gave him a smile that sent his blood pressure into the danger zone. "Not yet."

Reaching for the hem of her sweater, she held his gaze with hers, pulled the sweater over her head and tossed it on top of his clothes. He swallowed hard at the sight of her red lace bra. She unhooked the front closure, then slowly slipped if off her arms. His pulse pounded so hard in his ears, he thought he might go deaf. Her breasts seemed to be a little fuller than he remembered, the nipples a bit darker. He wanted to fill his hands with them, wanted to kiss and taste her until she begged for him to take her.

She popped the snap on her jeans, lowered the zipper and revealed the top of a pair of red lace panties to match her bra. Red had never looked so good to him. By the time she slid the denim down her thighs, sweat beaded his forehead and Brett felt as if he'd been set on fire.

"You're beautiful," he said, reaching for her.

She took his hands in hers and placed them on her shoulders. "Not yet, darling." She ran her fingers along the elastic waistband of his briefs. "I want you to remember tonight."

If he could have found his voice, he would have told her there was no danger he'd ever forget. But she was dipping her fingers below the band to slide his briefs off. He couldn't have strung a sentence together if his life depended on it.

Once she had the cotton tossed on top of the growing pile of his and her clothing, she took him in her small hands. Brett wasn't sure how much longer his legs would support him.

Her warm palms gently caressed and stroked him until he thought he might just start Chicago's next big fire. Taking her hands in his, he squeezed his eyes shut and fought for control. "I think...we'd better lie down," he choked out.

Treating him to the sexiest smile he'd ever hoped to see, she nodded and turned down the comforter. Brett stretched out and watched as Elena removed the scrap of red lace covering her, then joined him.

He immediately pulled her into his arms, and her soft body pressed to his sent desire sweeping through him with the force of a tidal wave. Unable to find the words to express how she made him feel, he worshipped her with his lips and hands.

Her full breasts filled his palms perfectly, the nipples beading in anticipation of his attention. Kissing his way down the slope of one creamy breast, he flicked his tongue across the tightly beaded peak, then drew it into his mouth. She moaned and tangled her fingers in his hair to hold him to her.

"Feel good?" he asked, raising his head to smile down at her.

"Yes."

He gave the same attention to her other breast. "Want me to stop?"

"If you do, I swear I'll arrest you for committing a criminal act," she said breathlessly.

He ran his hand down the smooth skin of her torso, then cupped the dark brown curls at the apex of her thighs. "And what crime would that be, sweet Elena?" he asked, parting her with one finger to stroke the tiny nub hidden within.

Her head pressed back against the pillow and she arched her lower body upward against his hand. "Failure to cooperate…with a police officer."

Brett tested her readiness with one finger. "Is the officer in need of assistance?" he murmured against her lips.

"Yes…she is."

Grinning, he nudged her knees apart and settled himself between her thighs. "Considering it's my civic duty, I'll be happy to do what I can. Could the officer tell me exactly what that might be?"

Her brown eyes sparkled with a hunger than made his body throb. "Make love to me, Brett."

"Honey, I thought you'd never ask," he said, pushing the blunt tip of his erection forward to slowly penetrate her warm, moist heat.

When she tilted her hips to take all of him, her slick body absorbed him into her until he wasn't sure where he ended and she began. So intense were the feelings coursing through him that he had to remind himself to breathe.

He pulled back, then once again pushed forward, setting a slow, easy pace that gained momentum and depth with each stroke. Every fiber of his being was tightening with the need to empty himself into her, but he fought to hang on to what slender thread of sanity he had left.

Her cry of need, the pleasured pain of her nails scoring his back, urged him to deepen his thrusts, to quicken the pace. He answered her demands and felt the waves of fulfillment ripple around him as she gave in to the storm raging within her.

Unable to hold back any longer, Brett's control snapped and he plunged into her, his body joining hers with the quaking spasms of released passion. His body pumped rhythmically, draining him of his essence, his strength. Losing the ability to support himself, he collapsed on top of her and buried his face in the pillow beside her head.

Several long moments later, reality finally returned and he quickly levered himself to Elena's side. Her eyes were closed and she lay so quiet, so still that his heart nearly stopped. If he'd hurt her...

"Elena, honey, are you all right?"

Her smile sent relief coursing through him. "I couldn't be better." She opened her eyes and wrapped her arms around his neck. "Unless, of course, you make love to me again."

He felt like beating his chest and yelling like Tarzan. "I think that can be arranged," he said, kissing her with all of the emotion he had welling up inside of him.

When he broke the kiss to nuzzle the sensitive hollow behind her ear, he felt her chest rise and fall as she took a deep breath. "I love you," she said quietly.

Brett went perfectly still. Had he heard her correctly? "What did you say?" he asked, propping himself on his forearms to stare down at her.

"I said—" She paused as if she weren't sure she should repeat it. "I said I love you."

The uncertainty reflected in her eyes tore at his insides. He had to tell her what he knew in his heart to be true. "I love you too, sweet Elena."

Several hours later, their arms twined around each other, they sat on the couch with Babe, watching the late-night news. Elena yawned and started to get up. "I really need to get home."

Brett shook his head. "Don't go."

She looked at the man she loved. She'd tried so hard not to care for him, but from the moment they met, Brett had made it impossible to resist him. "I can't. I don't have my clothes for work tomorrow and I—"

He placed his index finger to her lips. "Call in tomorrow and tell them—"

"I really can't stay." She placed a quick kiss on his lips, then, lifting Babe from her lap, Elena rose to her feet.

"I don't mean for you to tell them you're sick."

Brett stood up and took her into his arms. "I mean call and turn in your two-weeks' notice."

"I can't do that," she said, laughing. Surely he had to be joking.

"Sure you can. I've got it all worked out," he said, sounding quite pleased with himself.

It seemed as if her world came to a halt, and a tight knot formed in her stomach. "What do you mean you have it worked out?"

"The head of security at Connelly Corporation will be retiring this summer and I've arranged for you to take the job." Naming a ridiculously high sum of money that would be her salary he added, "And I want you to move in here with me and Babe."

Elena felt her heart shatter into a million pieces. "I have to go," she said, needing to get away from him.

She felt sick inside. How could Brett tell her he loved her and know so little about her? About what was important to her?

"What's wrong, honey?" he asked, sounding truly puzzled. He reached for her. "Do you want more money?"

She stopped to look at the hand he'd placed on her arm, then up at his confused expression. "You just don't get it, do you, Connelly?"

"Get what?"

"Me." She shook free of his grasp. "You don't have a clue how hard I've worked to be promoted to the SIU, or how important my career is to me."

"But—"

"But nothing." She poked his chest with her finger. "I'll bet *you* take pride in what you do as vice president of public relations."

He nodded, folded his arms and stared down at her. "Of course I do."

"Well, I'm no different." She paced the room. "I'm proud of the job I do and the fact that I'm good at it. And I'm also proud that I beat the odds and made something of myself when everything was stacked against me."

"I never doubted that you worked hard to get where you are," he said, sounding as if his patience was wearing thin. "But you're pregnant now and your job is dangerous. You've got to think of Peanut."

She stopped pacing to turn around and stare at him. "I am thinking of my child."

"But this will solve all your problems," he argued. "You can set your own hours at Connelly." He came to stand in front of her and, reaching out, placed his hands on her shoulders. "You won't miss out on all of Peanut's firsts." He pulled her into his arms. "And when you move in here with me and Babe, *I'll* be here to see all the firsts, too."

"I'm not taking the job, Brett." She pushed away from him. "And I'm not moving in with you."

He looked as if he couldn't quite grasp that she was turning down his offer. Propping his fists on his hips, he asked, "Why not?"

Tears blurred her vision. "You don't understand how much value I place on my independence or how much real commitment means to me."

"Yes, I do."

"No, you don't." She walked to the closet to get her coat. "If you did, you'd never have taken it upon yourself to arrange a job for me, nor would you have asked me to play house. Call me selfish, but I want it all.'' She stuffed her arms into her coat, then turned back to face him. ''I want the freedom and respect to make my own career choices. And I want the fairy tale. I want to belong to a family where love and commitment go hand in hand, where there's a happily-ever-after.''

''I do love you and Peanut,'' he insisted. ''And we can have those things.''

''No, Brett,'' she said sadly. ''It's not love if I'm the one making all the concessions. You need to learn that love isn't a matter of money or a job offer or playing house. It's far too valuable for that. I know that's a novel concept, and one that you've obviously never considered, but love is an emotional investment. To find real love and happiness, you have to invest the most valuable asset you have—yourself. You have to invest your heart and your soul.''

''I have.'' He ran his hand over the back of his neck as if to relieve the tension. ''I've never told another woman that I loved her, nor have I asked one to live with me.''

She sadly shook her head. ''You only think you love me, Brett.''

''How can you say that?'' he demanded. ''I'm doing everything in my power to show you.''

The tears flowed unchecked down her cheeks, but she didn't care. ''When love is real, you accept the person for who they are and what they value in life. You don't try to get them to change the career they've chosen or to ask them to accept an imitation of what they truly want in life.'' Her voice caught and she had to swallow hard before she could force words past the lump in her throat. ''I will always love you, Brett. But I'm not the woman for you.''

"Yes, you are, Elena." He looked as miserable as she felt, but she couldn't let it sway her. If he couldn't accept her for who she was, they had no future together.

Reaching down, she picked up the little dog whining at her feet. "Take care of him, Babe," she whispered.

Setting the animal back on the floor, Elena stared at him for several long moments. Her heart felt as if it were being torn from her body.

"Goodbye, Brett."

Eleven

Elena pulled the quilt up to her chin, curled into a ball and took a deep breath. She wouldn't shed another tear over Brett Connelly. She wouldn't.

But as she lay in bed, listening to the sounds of Chicago's early-morning traffic, moisture filled her eyes and ran down her cheeks. Why did she always fall for the wrong man?

With Michael she'd been young and had naively believed his empty promises. But she couldn't use that excuse with Brett. He hadn't promised anything. And it wasn't as though she hadn't tried to keep her distance with him.

But he'd been too strong a force to resist. He'd come into her life like a whirlwind and overwhelmed her with the sheer force of his personality. He'd taken it upon himself to befriend her when she'd needed someone the most. He'd been kind and caring, romantic and sentimental. How could she not fall in love with him?

She bit her lower lip to hold back the sobs. How was she going to be able to continue working on his brother's investigation? Brett was the Connelly family liaison, and she would have to meet with him occasionally to update them on her findings. How could she do that and not have her heart break each time she saw him?

And what would happen when she picked up the newspaper and read about him and another woman in the society columns? The first time she'd seen Michael's name mentioned as the escort of a well-known socialite to a charity ball, it hadn't bothered her one bit. But she knew for certain it would devastate her to see Brett's name linked with another woman's.

A wave of deep emotional pain swept through her at the mere thought of him with another woman, and Elena had to catch her breath to keep from crying out. She'd never loved Michael as completely as she'd loved Brett.

Squeezing her eyes shut, she willed herself to think. She had several very difficult decisions to make.

The walls suddenly seemed to close in, and unable to stay in bed another second, she threw back the covers and stumbled to her feet. She needed to get out of the apartment, out of Chicago.

Picking up the phone, she dialed her supervisor and arranged to take a few days off. That done, she grabbed a suitcase and began shoving clothes into it. She knew exactly where she needed to go and whom she needed to talk to in order to put her life back into perspective.

* * *

Fiona glared at him as he walked past her desk, and if looks could kill, Brett figured he'd be a dead man in short order. The woman had even stopped speaking to him by midmorning. His PR team wasn't any happier, either. They were ready to mutiny over his criticism of their latest proposal. And in the past two days Babe had torn up three more throw pillows and refused to acknowledge he even existed until it was time for him to take her for a walk.

Truth to tell, he couldn't blame them. Lately he didn't even like himself. In the two days since Elena walked out of his condo, he'd been in the worst mood of his life.

Staring at the papers on his desk, he tried for the thousandth time to figure out how he could have been such a fool. Instead of asking Elena if she'd be interested in taking the job with Connelly Corporation, he'd just thrown it at her. He'd been so damned arrogant and sure that she'd jump at the opportunity that he hadn't even considered how it would sound. He rubbed the tension knotting the back of his neck. He'd come across as if he thought her career was insignificant and worthless. It was no wonder she'd refused.

If that wasn't bad enough, he'd asked her to move in with him, instead of offering her the permanence of a commitment. And he'd known full well how important that was to her.

Hell, he couldn't have handled it worse if he'd tried.

Brett propped his elbows on the desk and rested his head in his hands. He'd never been this miserable in his entire life. He hadn't slept worth a damn the past two nights, and his appetite had disappeared completely. But those were easy to deal with compared to the ache in his chest. It felt as though someone had reached in and ripped his heart out.

He took a deep breath. Now he understood how Drew had felt when Talia died. Although they hadn't been madly in love, Drew had suffered terribly from her loss. And that was what Brett had tried to avoid by not getting too close to Elena.

But from the moment they met, he'd been drawn to her. He'd tried hard to convince himself that he just wanted to help her, to lend her moral support because she had no one else. But that had been an excuse, and a damned flimsy one. He'd never seen a more capable woman than Elena. She knew exactly what she wanted in life and she wasn't afraid to go after it.

No, the truth was that he was the one incapable of dealing with things. He'd fallen in love with her the moment he'd laid eyes on her, but he'd done everything in his power to try to deny it. He was the one who needed her, not the other way around.

So what are you going to do about it, Connelly?

He glanced at the phone. He'd tried calling her last night, but her machine had picked up and he'd figured she was screening calls to keep from having to talk to him. But if he called her at work, she'd have to talk to him.

Before he could think twice about what he would say to her, Brett picked up the phone and dialed SIU headquarters. When the switchboard operator put his call through, his palms started sweating and his mouth went dry.

"Detective Johnson," a man barked into Brett's ear.

"I'm trying to reach Detective Delgado," he said,

his impatience mounting now that he knew exactly what he wanted to do.

"Sorry, she's not in. Want to leave a message?"

Disappointment stabbed at Brett's gut. "This is Brett Connelly. Would you have her call me when she gets back?"

"Does this have something to do with the Daniel Connelly case?" the man asked.

"Yes, it does," Brett lied. He figured if Elena thought his call had something to do with the investigation, he'd have a better chance of setting up a meeting with her.

"I can take the information," Detective Johnson said.

"No, I'd rather speak with Detective Delgado," Brett insisted, making sure his voice carried a no-nonsense edge to it.

"She took some time off and won't be back until sometime next week," Johnson said.

Brett felt as if the floor dropped from beneath him. "Is she all right?" Had their arguing caused her to have problems with Peanut?

"Far as I know, she's fine. She said something about visiting a relative or friend or something." The man's blasé attitude grated on Brett's nerves.

"Do you know if she left town?" Brett demanded, knowing of only one person she might be going to see.

"Look, buddy, I don't get paid to keep track of who leaves town and who doesn't." Detective Johnson sounded more than a little annoyed. "All I know is she had vacation days built up and decided to take some time off. Now, if you have something to add to the Connelly case, I can take the information. Otherwise, she'll call you when she gets back next week.''

"Thanks,'' Brett said when the man hung up on him. There was no way he'd wait that long to talk to Elena.

Dialing Lake Shore Manor, he asked Ruby to put him through to one of his parents. He wanted to make sure they knew how to get hold of him in case there was another development.

When his mother came on the line, she sounded as if she'd been crying. What the hell else could have happened? he wondered.

"What's wrong, Mom?''

"Brett, it's good to hear from you. How are you, darling?'' his mother asked, her manners as impeccable as always.

"I'm fine.'' He took a deep breath to keep from sounding as impatient as he felt. He wanted to get on the road. "Why are you crying, Mom?''

"Your cousin, Princess Catherine, called to say she's delaying her visit,'' Emma said, sniffling.

"Did she say why?'' Brett asked as he started clearing his desk.

"She mentioned something about finding questionable papers in her father's belongings.'' Emma's voice caught. "This is all so upsetting.''

Brett understood how hard it was for his mother. Having one of her sons be the target in an assassination attempt was bad enough, but learning that her father and brother were quite possibly the victims of the same assassin had to be devastating.

"Did she say what kind of papers they were?'' Brett asked.

"No, darling. Just that they were somehow tied to Sheikh Kaj al bin Russard."

"Who's he?" Brett asked, snapping his briefcase closed.

He heard his mother sniff back more tears before she went on. "He's the new prince of Walburaq. He's on his way to Altaria for a state visit and asked to speak to Catherine privately. She's hoping he might have answers about the papers."

"Be sure to let me know if she finds out anything," Brett said, thinking that what his cousin learned might help Elena with Daniel's case.

"I will."

Before his mother could start speculating on what the sheikh knew about the mysterious papers, Brett said, "Listen, Mom, I'm going out of town for a few days. If you need me for anything, I can be reached on my cell phone."

"Of course, darling," Emma said. "Do be careful, Brett. With everything that's taken place—"

"I will, Mom," he promised. "I'll call when I get back in town."

Hanging up the phone, Brett gathered his coat and briefcase, his mind already on Elena and his plan of action. He'd have to go by her apartment to be sure, but he had a hunch that he'd be headed down state before the day was over.

"Elena, honey, it sounds like somebody's at the door," Marie Waters said, kneading a large ball of bread dough. "Would you see who it is?"

"Sure." Elena put down the knife she'd been using to chop carrots and wiped her hands on a towel. "It's probably your friend Mr. Quimby."

"If it is, tell the old goat to pack his papers else-where." Marie pounded the dough. "I'm not lookin' for him or any other man to fill my time."

Elena smiled as she walked to the front door and turned on the porch light. Some things never changed. Mr. Quimby had been trying to get Marie to go out with him for as long as Elena had known them, and Marie still wouldn't give the poor old gentleman the time of day. When Elena asked her why, Marie had pointed out that she'd been married to her late hus-band for forty years and she wasn't about to settle for second best now that the love of her life was gone.

Looking out the peephole, Elena didn't see anyone on the other side. "Are you sure you heard some-one?" she called to Marie.

Before her foster mother could respond, Elena heard a light tap, then a definite thump. It sounded as if it came from the side of the house instead of the other side of the door. Probably one of the neighbors' children bouncing a ball against the side of the ga-rage, she decided. But she opened the door just to make sure.

Blinking, she couldn't believe her eyes. A small black ball of hair danced and yipped happily at her feet. "Babe?" Elena said incredulously. She picked up the wiggling little dog. "How did you—" She stopped abruptly and looked around. "Where's Brett?"

"Right here," he said, stepping from the twilight shadows to climb the porch steps. He held one hand behind him.

"Why are you here?" she demanded, hugging Babe close.

She'd traveled over three hundred miles in order to

put things in perspective, to get away from him so she could decide what she had to do to survive life without him. Now here he stood looking so handsome and sexy he stole her breath.

"Could I come inside?" he asked, pulling a bouquet of red roses from behind his back.

Elena shook her head. "I don't think that would be a good idea, Brett."

He stepped closer. "Why not?" Touching her cheek with his finger, he traced a line down to her chin. "I think we need to settle a few things between us."

She set Babe on her feet, then took a step backward. "We said all there was to say the other night at your condo."

Brett shook his head. "You might have, but I didn't."

"Who's at the door, Elena?" Marie asked, coming from the kitchen to stand at Elena's shoulder. Her curious gaze raked Brett from head to toe. "You look a little too old to be sellin' candy to raise money for the high school band, so I assume you're the young man who put the shadows under Elena's eyes."

"I'm afraid you're right," Brett said. "And I'm sorry about that. But I've driven all the way from Chicago to try to make things right."

"I would hope so," the little woman said, nodding her head until her short white curls bobbed. She glanced down at Babe. "And who is this little sweetie?"

"My dog." One glance at Elena's disapproving look and he decided not to elaborate. "I call her Babe."

"She's a real cutie," the woman said, bending down to pick up his dog.

Brett liked Marie Waters immediately. "With your

permission, Mrs. Waters, I'd like to come in and speak with Elena.''

The woman nodded her approval as she patted the top of Babe's head. ''That would be up to her, young man.'' Turning to Elena, Marie asked, ''How do you feel about him joinin' us for supper?''

Elena didn't look happy about it, but she finally shrugged. ''I don't mind if you don't, Marie.''

''Then it's settled.'' The woman took the bouquet of roses he still held, then, holding both the flowers and his dog, turned to go back into the house. ''Me and Babe are goin' to the kitchen to find her a treat and put these pretty flowers in a vase while you two young folks settle your differences.''

Taking a deep breath, Brett followed the two women inside and closed the door. He'd made it over the first hurdle. He at least had the chance to talk to Elena.

While Marie and Babe disappeared down a hall, Elena walked over to the couch and sat down. Her body language shouted that she was on the defensive, and he knew for certain he'd have a hard time convincing her of his sincerity.

He purposely remained standing. He had too much pent-up energy to sit still. This was the most important moment of his life, and he didn't want to blow it.

''Before you say anything, I want you to promise me you'll hear me out.''

She stared at him for several long seconds, and the hurt he saw reflected in her big brown eyes twisted his gut and made him want to rush his appeal. ''Brett, I can't do this,'' she said, her voice shaky. ''Please make your apologies to Marie, take Babe and leave.''

He shook his head. "No. I can't just walk away and let go of what we have."

"We don't have anything," she said, shaking her head.

"Yes, we do." He wasn't about to let her deny the best thing that had ever happen to either of them. "We love each other."

"Brett—"

He watched tears fill her eyes, and the thought that he'd caused her such pain tightened the knot in his stomach. "Just give me five minutes, Elena. If I can't convince you to give us another chance, then I promise I'll leave."

She stared at him for endless seconds, and just when he thought she was going to refuse his request, she nodded. "Five minutes, Connelly. That's it."

His relief was almost staggering. Unable to stand still any longer, he began to pace. "There's something you need to understand, Elena. I've never felt like this before." He stopped in front of her. "I've never found myself in the position of being so consumed by wanting to make another person happy that—" He took a deep breath. It wasn't easy for him to admit there was an area where he was unsure of himself, but this was too important to mince words. "I'm not real sure of what to do. Or how to go about doing it."

When she remained silent, he went on. "I want you to know right up front that I do respect your career even though it scares the hell out of me to think of you having to investigate criminals."

"I can take care of myself."

He nodded. "I know that. But it doesn't keep me from worrying about you."

"Most of my job consists of taking statements and

filing reports,'' she said, staring down at her tightly clasped hands. ''We're usually called after a crime has been committed.''

Her small reassurance gave him hope. At least she was listening to him. ''That makes me feel a little better. And I promise from now on to discuss things with you instead of trying to take matters into my own hands.''

''How do you know there will be a next time?'' she asked.

''That's why I'm here, Elena,'' he said, swallowing his pride. ''I'm begging you to give us—give me—another chance.''

''But do you think you could ever accept that I'm going to keep my job with SIU? Respect the fact that it's my career? My choice?''

''It will always be a source of worry for me,'' he said honestly. ''But, yes, I promise to trust your judgment and training.''

''You wouldn't try to pressure me into taking the job with Connelly Corporation?'' she asked.

''No. No more pressure.''

She looked up at him and he knew what was running through her mind. He hadn't mentioned anything about their relationship. He took a deep breath. He felt as if he was about to leap off a cliff.

''I want you to understand something about me, Elena. Until now I haven't had any experience with the give and take of a relationship, of talking things over and coming to a compromise.'' He shook his head. ''And, I have to admit, until I met you, I really hadn't cared to gain any.''

''Why not?''

Rubbing the knot of tension at the back of his neck,

Brett searched for the right words. How could he explain how he'd felt without sounding like a coward? Would she understand that he hadn't wanted to hand over his heart and risk being hurt? Or worse yet, end up hurting the woman he loved?

"Until now, I wasn't interested in learning about commitment because the Connellys don't exactly have an exemplary track record when it comes to relationships," he said honestly. "Even my mom and dad had problems and almost divorced after my brother Rafe was born."

"I remember that coming out during the interviews," Elena said.

Brett nodded. "My half brother Seth, was born during that time, and although my mother came to love him, it was really hard for her to get over my father being with another woman." He knelt down in front of Elena and took her hands in his. "I know this is going to sound crazy, but I never want to hurt the woman I love that way."

"I don't think you would, Brett," she said, her voice little more than a whisper. "You're too kind, too caring for that."

Her words gave him hope that she understood what he was trying to tell her. But would she understand that he'd also avoided involvement because he didn't want to suffer the same kind of hurt that Drew had when Talia died?

"There's something else," he said.

"What's that?" she asked softly.

"When I realized your job held even a hint of danger, all I could think about was the hell Drew went through when his wife died." Brett took a deep breath. "Drew survived, but I know as surely as I breathe air that if something happened to you, I couldn't go on. You're my heart, Elena. My soul." His voice shook with emotion, but he didn't care. "Can you find it in your heart to forgive me and give us another chance?"

Tears ran down her cheeks. "You're not the only one who's afraid, Brett."

Wrapping his arms around her, he held her close. "I know, honey. But I'm willing to take the chance if you are. I can't live without you. I want us to get married and spend the rest of our lives together."

She pulled back, looking uncertain. "You won't have a problem with the fact that the baby I'm carrying—"

He placed his finger against her lips to stop what she was about to ask. "I love Peanut. I already think of him—"

"Her," Elena corrected, giving him a smile that warmed his soul. "I keep telling you, this baby is a girl."

Brett grinned. "I already think of *her* as mine. I want to be there with you when you give birth to Peanut. I want to be the man she calls Daddy. And years from now if she can ever find a boy I think is worthy of my daughter, I want to walk her down the aisle at her wedding."

"Really, Brett? Do you mean it?"

"Honey, I love you. You're my everything and I want to be yours," he said, feeling he'd been set free with the admission. "Will you marry me?"

"Yes," she said, laughing and crying at the same time. "But only on one condition."

He didn't think the stipulation would be too bad, since she was laughing. "What's that, honey?"

"You have to change the dog's name from Babe Magnet to just Babe."

"Not a problem," he said, laughing. Her tears continued and he had to ask, "These are some of those happy tears, right?"

She nodded. "Why?"

"Just checking." Taking her hand in his, he rose to his feet and pulled her up with him. "Let's go see if Marie puts her stamp of approval on all this."

Elena gave him a kiss that made his body tighten and his heart hammer against his ribs. "You already have it. Otherwise, she would have never let you in the house."

He looked thoughtful. "You know that's something we'd better consider."

She looked thoroughly confused. "What are you talking about?"

"A house." He smiled and place his hand on the gentle roundness of her stomach. "We're going to need a big house with lots of bedrooms and a big yard for Peanut and the rest of the kids to play in."

"Uh, Brett, how many children are we talking about?" she asked. "Morning sickness isn't exactly a picnic in the park."

"Six or eight." He loved the idea of being a husband and father. "You choose."

"I'd be pregnant all the time," she said, laughing.

"Maternally mine," he said, kissing the tip of her nose.

Elena wrapped her arms around him and, nodding, gave him a smile that lit the darkest corners of his soul. "Maternally yours."

* * * * *

DYNASTIES: THE CONNELLYS

King Thomas Rosemere (d) m. Queen Lucinda (d)

Sonia Anton

Prince Marc Rosemere (d)

Princess Emma Rosemere m. Grant Connelly

Tobias Connelly m. Lilly

③ Princess Catherine Rosemere*

④ Chance Barnett-Connelly*

⑤ Douglas Barnett-Connelly*

Twins

Hannah Barnett

Angie Donahue

⑩ Seth Connelly*

① Daniel Connelly (heir apparent) m. Erin Lawrence

⑪ Raïe Connelly

⑦ Alexandra Connelly

⑥ Justin Connelly

② Brett Connelly m. Elena Delgado

⑧ Drew Connelly 1st m. Talia Van Dorn (d)

Amanda Connelly

⑨ Tara Connelly

⑫ Maggie Connelly

Twins

① Tall, Dark & Royal
② Maternally Yours
③ The Sheikh Takes a Bride
④ The SEAL's Surrender
⑤ Plain Jane & Doctor Dad
⑥ And the Winner Gets...Married!
⑦ The Royal & the Runaway Bride
⑧ His E-Mail Order Wife
⑨ The Secret Baby Bond
⑩ Cinderella's Convenient Husband
⑪ Expecting...and in Danger
⑫ Cherokee Marriage Dare

Symbols:
- - - - Affair
* Child of an Affair
(d) Deceased

Look for the story of
Princess Catherine of Altaria
and Sheikh Kaj al bin Russard in

THE SHEIKH TAKES A BRIDE

by Caroline Cross
Book 3 (SD 1424) in the
exciting new miniseries,

Dynasties: The Connellys

On sale March 2002

For a sneak preview,
turn the page…

One

"**Y**ou're absolutely right, Kaj," Joffrey Dunstan, Earl of Alston, said in his usual thoughtful way. "She's even lovelier than I remembered."

Glancing away from the slim, auburn-haired young woman who was the subject of his observation, the earl retreated a step from the balcony railing overlooking the grand ballroom of Altaria Palace. Though more than two hundred members of Europe's elite milled down below in their most elegant evening wear, they might not have existed for all the attention he gave them.

Instead, with a bemused expression on his face, he turned to stare at his companion, who stood in a pocket of shadow, hidden from casual observance. "But marriage? You can't be serious."

Sheikh Kaj al bin Russard raised an ink-black eyebrow in question. "And why is that?"

"Because... That is..." Always the diplomat, Joffrey cleared his throat and tried again. "Surely you're aware that Princess Catherine has a certain...reputation. And Sheikh Tarik's will was quite specific—"

"That I marry a virgin of royal blood." Kaj grimaced. "Have a little faith, cousin. I haven't forgotten my father's unfortunate directive. I'd simply remind you that for all Catherine's reputedly wild ways, there's a reason she's known as the Ice Princess."

"I suppose you have a point. Still..."

Kaj took one last look at the woman he intended to marry, his hooded gray eyes admiring her chestnut hair and slim white shoulders before he turned his full attention to his favorite relative.

"If it will ease your mind, Joff, I've made certain inquiries. The princess may be a tease, but she's no trollop. On the contrary, I have it on excellent authority that her virtue is very much intact. Her pleasure seems to come from keeping her admirers at arms length."

Joffrey's eyes widened in sudden comprehension. "You see her as a challenge!"

Kaj gave a light shrug, broad shoulders lifting. "If I have to marry, I might at least enjoy the courtship, don't you think?"

"No, I most certainly do not," the other man retorted. "At least not to the exclusion of more important considerations."

Kaj crossed his arms. "And those would be what, exactly?"

"Compatibility. Mutual respect and understanding. Similar values. And—love." A faint flush of embarrassed color tinted the earl's cheeks at that last word, but his gaze was steady as he plowed stubbornly on.

"This isn't a prize to be won, Kaj. This is your life, your future. Your happiness."

"Do you think I don't know that?" the sheikh inquired softly. "Trust me. I have no intention of making my parents's mistakes."

Joffrey looked instantly stricken, as well he should since he was one of the few people who understood the price Kaj had paid for Lady Helena Spenser's and Sheikh Tarik al bin Russard's disastrous marriage, bitter divorce and subsequent flurry of heated affairs. "Of course not. I didn't mean to imply you did. It's just that this hardly seems the answer."

"And what is?" Kaj's voice was studiously polite. "Given the need for my bride to be physically pristine, what are my choices? Should I marry one of those tremulous debutantes your mother keeps throwing into my path? Or should I make an offer for some Walbarqui chieftain's daughter, a sheltered innocent who'll build her whole life around me?" He sighed. "I don't want that, Joff. I want a woman who's pragmatic enough to see a union with me as a mutually beneficial partnership. Not some starry-eyed romantic who'll fall desperately in love with me and expect me to fulfill her every wish and need."

"Well, if it's any consolation, I doubt excess worship of you will be a problem with Princess Catherine," he said, matching Kaj's tone.

Kaj cocked his head in feigned interest. "Do tell."

The earl shrugged, "It's simply that the more I think about it, the more I understand your choice. Unlike every other female on the planet, the princess has never shown the slightest tendency to swoon when you walk into the room. And though she may indeed be a virgin—I bow to your superior sources—

she doesn't strike me as the kind of woman who'll ever fall at your feet in girlish devotion. As a matter of fact—'' he glanced down at the ballroom spread out below them ''—you'll probably be lucky to get a date.''

Kaj followed his gaze. He quickly noted that Altaria's new kind, Daniel Connelly, was about to kick off the dancing with his queen, Erin. Of more immediate interest to him, however, was the discovery that the crush of young men vying for Princess Catherine's attention had grown even larger than before. He felt an unexpected pinch of irritation as one would-be swain said something that made her laugh. Vowing to put an end to such familiarity—soon—he nevertheless refused to rise to his cousin's bait.

Catherine *would* be his. He'd given a great deal of thought to her selection, and one way or another he always got what he wanted.

*   *   *   *   *

You are invited to enter the
exclusive, masculine
world of the...

TEXAS
Cattleman's Club
The Last Bachelor

Silhouette Desire's powerful miniseries
features five wealthy Texas bachelors—all
members of the state's most prestigious club—
who set out to uncover a traitor in their midst...
and discover their true loves!

THE MILLIONAIRE'S PREGNANT BRIDE
by Dixie Browning
February 2002 (SD #1420)

HER LONE STAR PROTECTOR
by Peggy Moreland
March 2002 (SD #1426)

TALL, DARK...AND FRAMED?
by Cathleen Galitz
April 2002 (SD #1433)

THE PLAYBOY MEETS HIS MATCH
by Sara Orwig
May 2002 (SD #1438)

THE BACHELOR TAKES A WIFE
by Jackie Merritt
June 2002 (SD #1444)

Available at your favorite retail outlet.

Silhouette®
Where love comes alive™

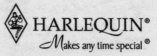

This Mother's Day Give Your Mom A Royal Treat

Win a fabulous one-week vacation in Puerto Rico for you and your mother at the luxurious Inter-Continental San Juan Resort & Casino. The prize includes round trip airfare for two, breakfast daily and a mother and daughter day of beauty at the beachfront hotel's spa.

INTER·CONTINENTAL
San Juan
RESORT & CASINO

Here's all you have to do:

Tell us in 100 words or less how your mother helped with the romance in your life. It may be a story about your engagement, wedding or those boyfriends when you were a teenager or any other romantic advice from your mother. The entry will be judged based on its originality, emotionally compelling nature and sincerity.
See official rules on following page.

Send your entry to:
Mother's Day Contest

In Canada
P.O. Box 637
Fort Erie, Ontario
L2A 5X3

In U.S.A.
P.O. Box 9076
3010 Walden Ave.
Buffalo, NY
14269-9076

Or enter online at www.eHarlequin.com

PRROY

HARLEQUIN MOTHER'S DAY CONTEST 2216
OFFICIAL RULES
NO PURCHASE NECESSARY TO ENTER

Two ways to enter:

- **Via The Internet:** Log on to the Harlequin romance website (www.eHarlequin.com) anytime beginning 12:01 a.m. E.S.T., January 1, 2002 through 11:59 p.m. E.S.T., April 1, 2002 and follow the directions displayed on-line to enter your name, address (including zip code), e-mail address and in 100 words or fewer, describe how your mother helped with the romance in your life.

- **Via Mail:** Handprint (or type) on an 8 1/2" x 11" plain piece of paper, your name, address (including zip code) and e-mail address (if you have one), and in 100 words or fewer, describe how your mother helped with the romance in your life. Mail your entry via first-class mail to: Harlequin Mother's Day Contest 2216, (in the U.S.) P.O. Box 9076, Buffalo, NY 14269-9076; (in Canada) P.O. Box 637, Fort Erie, Ontario, Canada L2A 5X3.

For eligibility, entries must be submitted either through a completed Internet transmission or postmarked no later than 11:59 p.m. E.S.T., April 1, 2002 (mail-in entries must be received by April 9, 2002). Limit one entry per person, household address and e-mail address. On-line and/or mailed entries received from persons residing in geographic areas in which entry is not permissible will be disqualified.

Entries will be judged by a panel of judges, consisting of members of the Harlequin editorial, marketing and public relations staff using the following criteria:
- Originality - 50%
- Emotional Appeal - 25%
- Sincerity - 25%

In the event of a tie, duplicate prizes will be awarded. Decisions of the judges are final.

Prize: A 6-night/7-day stay for two at the Inter-Continental San Juan Resort & Casino, including round-trip coach air transportation from gateway airport nearest winner's home (approximate retail value: $4,000). Prize includes breakfast daily and a mother and daughter day of beauty at the beachfront hotel's spa. Prize consists of data these items listed as part of the prize. Prize is valued in U.S. currency.

All entries become the property of Torstar Corp. and will not be returned. No responsibility is assumed for lost, late, illegible, incomplete, inaccurate, non-delivered or misdirected mail or misdirected e-mail, for technical, hardware or software failures of any kind, lost or unavailable network connections, or failed, incomplete, garbled or delayed computer transmission or any human error which may occur in the receipt or processing of the entries in this Contest.

Contest open only to residents of the U.S. (except Colorado) and Canada, who are 18 years of age or older and is void wherever prohibited by law; all applicable laws and regulations apply. Any litigation within the Province of Quebec respecting the conduct or organization of a publicity contest may be submitted to the Régie des alcools, des courses et des jeux for a ruling. Any litigation respecting the awarding of a prize may be submitted to the Régie des alcools, des courses et des jeux only for the purpose of helping the parties reach a settlement. Employees and immediate family members of Torstar Corp. and D.L. Blair, Inc., their affiliates, subsidiaries and all other agencies, entities and persons connected with the use, marketing or conduct of this Contest are not eligible to enter. Taxes on prize are the sole responsibility of winner. Acceptance of any prize offered constitutes permission to use winner's name, photograph or other likeness for the purposes of advertising, trade and promotion on behalf of Torstar Corp., its affiliates and subsidiaries without further compensation to the winner, unless prohibited by law.

Winner will be determined no later than April 15, 2002 and be notified by mail. Winner will be required to sign and return an Affidavit of Eligibility form within 15 days after winner notification. Non-compliance within that time period may result in disqualification and an alternate winner may be selected. Winner of trip must execute a Release of Liability prior to ticketing and must possess required travel documents (e.g. Passport, photo ID) where applicable. Travel must be completed within 12 months of selection and is subject to traveling companion completing and returning a Release of Liability prior to travel; and hotel and flight accommodations availability. Certain restrictions and blackout dates may apply. No substitution of prize permitted by winner. Torstar Corp. and D.L. Blair, Inc., their parents, affiliates, and subsidiaries are not responsible for errors in printing or electronic presentation of Contest, or entries. In the event of printing or other errors which may result in unintended prize values or duplication of prizes, all affected entries shall be null and void. If for any reason the Internet portion of the Contest is not capable of running as planned, including infection by computer virus, bugs, tampering, unauthorized intervention, fraud, technical failures, or any other causes beyond the control of Torstar Corp. which corrupt or affect the administration, secrecy, fairness, integrity or proper conduct of the Contest, Torstar Corp. reserves the right, at its sole discretion, to disqualify any individual who tampers with the entry process and to cancel, terminate, modify or suspend the Contest or the Internet portion thereof. In the event the Internet portion must be terminated a notice will be posted on the website and all entries received prior to termination will be judged in accordance with these rules. In the event of a dispute regarding an on-line entry, the entry will be deemed submitted by the authorized holder of the e-mail account submitted at the time of entry. Authorized account holder is defined as the natural person who is assigned to an e-mail address by an Internet access provider, on-line service provider or other organization that is responsible for arranging e-mail address for the domain associated with the submitted e-mail address. Torstar Corp. and/or D.L. Blair Inc. assumes no responsibility for any computer injury or damage related to or resulting from accessing and/or downloading any sweepstakes material. Rules are subject to any requirements/limitations imposed by the FCC. Purchase or acceptance of a product offer does not improve your chances of winning.

For winner's name (available after May 1, 2002), send a self-addressed, stamped envelope to: Harlequin Mother's Day Contest Winners 2216, P.O. Box 4200 Blair, NE 68009-4200 or you may access the www.eHarlequin.com Web site through June 3, 2002.

Contest sponsored by Torstar Corp., P.O. Box 9042, Buffalo, NY 14269-9042.

Silhouette Desire®

presents

DYNASTIES: THE CONNELLYS

A brand-new miniseries about the Connellys of Chicago, a wealthy, powerful American family tied by blood to the royal family of the island kingdom of Altaria. They're wealthy, powerful and rocked by scandal, betrayal…and passion!

Look for a whole year of glamorous and utterly romantic tales in 2002:

Silhouette®

Where love comes alive™